Three Girls
and
a
Leading Man

Rachel Schurig

For Andrea.

Twenty-plus years and still going strong. Thank you for everything!

ACKNOWLEDGMENTS

Special thanks to Andrea, Angie, Mary, and Michelle
for your help and advice.

Thank you to my family and friends who have been so
supportive of this series.

Thank you to Nicolas J. Ambrose for editing services.

Book cover design by Scarlett Rugers Design 2011

www.scarlettrugers.com

Chapter One

*'Are you feeling lonely? Depressed? Hopeless? As the years go by are you finding that more and more of your friends are getting married and leaving you behind? Are you tired of being the only single girl? Don't despair—there's hope for you yet! You've taken an important first step in buying this book. Together, we'll discover what's holding you back from the happiness you deserve.'—**The Single Girl's Guide to Finding True Love***

"She has got to be kidding me," I muttered, staring down at the book in my hands in disgust.

"What's up?" Jen asked, peering over the top of her laptop.

"My mother," I said, sighing. "She's sent me a *gift.*"

"What is it?"

"Seriously, Jen, you don't even want to know."

I threw the book, along with the rest of the mail I had just brought in, down on the dining room table and walked into the kitchen to pour myself a drink.

"Wow, Annie," Jen called from the living room. "If you need a drink before you've even taken your shoes off or set your purse down, that must have been one heck of a present."

After a moment's search, I found a half-empty bottle of chardonnay in the fridge. "Thank God," I muttered, turning to the cabinet to find a wine glass. Empty. Of course. I pulled open the dishwasher, where I had loaded several glasses the night before, to find it full—but still unwashed.

"Damn it, Tina," I muttered, slamming the washer closed. My irritation was growing by the minute now, and my roommate Tina's inability to do the simplest thing was so not helping. It was Friday night, I'd had a long week at work, and I just wanted a glass of wine. Was that too much to ask?

"Hey, pour me some," Jen called.

A minute later I joined my best friend in the living room.

"Classy," she said, raising her eyebrows as I handed her a coffee mug full of chardonnay.

"It was the only thing that was clean," I told her, sitting next to her on the couch. "Tina didn't run the dishwasher after her little gathering last night."

Jen groaned. "That girl is on my last nerve."

Tina was our third roommate. She'd been living with us for the last six months. To say we weren't crazy about her would be an understatement.

"She had those people here until two a.m. last night," Jen continued. "Chanting and doing God knows what with those crystals."

"Let's just kick her out," I said, plopping my feet up on the coffee table.

Jen laughed. "If we could afford the rent, I would in a second. I'd be happy to be rid of the incense and the mess and the constant references to my aura." Jen pushed her dark hair out of her eyes. "Do you know that last week she told me my prana was murky? What does that even mean?"

I rolled my eyes and took a long pull of my wine.

"How was your day?" Jen asked. I closed my eyes. My day had been *long*. "That good, huh?"

"Same old crap," I said. "Stuck in the office doing busy work while Grayson got to do all the creative stuff. Just what I always dreamed I'd be doing when I went to work in theater."

Jen winced. "I'm sorry, hon," she said. "Want to talk about it?"

"What's there to say? My job is lame and pays me next to nothing."

We were distracted from this depressing topic by the sound of someone at the front door. Whoever it was, they seemed to be having a difficult time getting the door open.

"A little help?" called a familiar voice from the porch.

I jumped up and ran to the door, throwing it open to reveal our other best friend, Ginny, standing on the porch with her arms full and a small child by her legs tugging on her sweater.

"Gin!" I said happily. "I didn't know you were coming over!"

"Grab the baby, would you?" she asked, shifting the load in her hands.

I scooped Danny up, kissing him. "Hey, buddy!"

"Annie, Annie!" he squealed, and I felt my heart soar.

Besides Ginny and Jen, whom I had been best friends with forever, Danny was the most important person in my life. It had been a shock, sure, when Ginny told us she was pregnant at the age of twenty-three. And, yes, it *had* been super scary dealing with the birth and having a newborn baby around. But I wouldn't change any of it for anything. Because now we had Danny.

I stepped aside to make room for Ginny to come inside, bringing Danny over to the couch and swinging him around and down into Jen's arms. He laughed and reached for her and I saw her face light up, too. God, the kid had us wrapped around his little finger.

"I'm glad you're both home," Ginny said, dropping Danny's diaper bag and folded up pack-and-play on the floor. "I was hoping to hide out here tonight."

I smiled, glad that Ginny didn't feel the need to ask for our permission. This used to be her house, too. The three of us had found it after graduating from college and rented it together. Ginny had found out about the baby right there in our kitchen, and this had been Danny's first home.

"Yay!" Jen said, tickling Danny's belly. "Sleepover!"

"What are you hiding out from?" I asked.

Ginny rolled her eyes. "Josh is having a fantasy football draft at our house. Can you believe that? Ten grown men pretending that they have actual football teams. Drinking beer and smoking cigars like they think they're so cool. It's just too lame for words. I had to get out."

I laughed, rather nastily, and Jen shot me a warning look. I had a bit of a history of disliking Ginny's husband, Josh, but I was over it now. Mostly.

"Well, I'm glad you're here," I told her. "Jen and I were just having some wine."

"Ooh, that reminds me," Gin said, bending down and rummaging through Danny's diaper bag. "I brought us some pinot!"

Jen and I both laughed. It was so Ginny to carry wine around in her baby's diaper bag.

"How 'bout I make us some dinner?" Jen said, getting to her feet. "What do you guys feel like? I think

I have some pesto; we could do a chicken and pasta thing."

Ginny moaned. Jen was a fabulous cook.

Looking around the room, I felt my spirits rise. I might be totally frustrated in my job, live with a psycho like Tina, and have a mother that drove me crazy, but tonight, it didn't matter. My two best friends were here. What else did I need?

Chapter Two

An hour and a half later, the three of us sat down at the dining room table. While Jen had cooked, Ginny and I had fed Danny, given him his bath, and set him up in my bedroom in his pack-and-play for the night.

"Freedom," Ginny said, raising her wine glass (I had begrudgingly run the dishwasher). "No baby, no men, no jobs. It's the weekend, girls."

"Thank God," I said, downing my pinot quickly. "This week was hella lame."

"Annie is having a shitty time at work," Jen explained to Ginny.

Gin made a face at me. "Sorry, hon. What's up?"

"I'm just...bored. I never wanted to work in an office and it feels like that's all I do."

On paper, my job was perfect. I worked at Springwells Theater Company, an awesome small, non-profit theater in Detroit, about twenty minutes away from our house in Ferndale. We ran a lot of programs for teens and kids—play writing, acting, dance, things like that. I loved that part of my job—but more and more I was being shunted off into the office to do busywork. Administrative crap was really not my thing.

"I went into theater so I could be creative," I said, pouring myself more wine. "But it feels like I sit at a desk all day dealing with soul-crushing, administrative bullshit."

"Well," Jen said, dishing me out some pesto pasta. "Are there any auditions on the horizon?"

I had to roll my eyes a little. Just like Jen to bring it back to the positive, no matter how grouchy I was acting.

"Actually, there is. A really cool new show has open calls next week." I paused for effect. "It's being produced by Jenner Collins."

"Oooh," Ginny said. "Big time!"

Jenner Collins was a native Detroiter who had made it big in Hollywood. He'd even been nominated for a Golden Globe a few years ago. When he wasn't hanging out in L.A. being a big-time movie star, he spent part of his time back in Detroit, producing new plays with local talent. Getting into one of his shows would be a dream come true.

I'd wanted to be an actress for as long as I could remember. There was nothing I loved more than getting up on stage and completely losing myself in a character. My friends have always said I have a flair for the dramatic; I guess it makes sense that I chose drama as my career.

A lot of old friends from college question why I still live around here. Detroit isn't necessarily the place to be if you want to be a star. When I told my mother I was majoring in drama, she burst into tears, assuming it meant I would be moving out to L.A. to try to break into movies. "You'll end up living in a slum and taking your top off for money!" she had sobbed.

What most people didn't seem to understand is that I had no interest in the fame thing. Sure, I would love to act on stage on Broadway, or something, but I wasn't going to uproot my life over it. I was happy in Detroit—it was an awesome city with a great arts scene. People were putting up cool, edgy shows all over the place. I would be happy if I could make a living working around here, even if it meant I never made it to Broadway. Besides, the girls lived here.

What I had never realized is that it's every bit as hard to find your big break in Detroit as it is a big city like New York.

"Well, I think you should go for it," Ginny said, reaching over to move a pile of mail a bit farther from her plate. "Let me know if you need help running lines."

"Thanks," I said. This is what I loved about my friends—they always took my passion seriously. Never once had they told me I should move on and find a real job.

"Hey, what's this?" Gin asked, pulling a book off the pile of mail she had just moved. "*The Single Girl's Guide to Finding True Love*?"

I groaned. "My mother sent it."

Ginny started laughing as she flipped through the book. "Oh, my. This is ridiculously sad."

"Tell me about it," I grumbled, helping myself to more of Jen's pasta concoction. "That woman just has no clue."

"Aw, she means well," Jen said. "She just wants you to be happy."

"And apparently, being happy requires you to follow these 'Ten simple steps to making the right impression on your first date'," Ginny said, pointing to a random page in the book. "Oh, no. I'm starting to see where you're going wrong, sweetie. According to this you should always let the man lead the conversation and should only talk about yourself in response to his specific questions."

Jen snorted. "That sounds just like you, Ann."

"You also should never, ever ask a man out and should only kiss someone after three dates."

"If that's what it takes to land a guy, you're screwed," Jen said with a smirk.

"I doubt I would have much interest in any guy that would care about shit like that," I replied. "When was that book written, anyhow? 1950?"

Ginny flipped to the front cover.

"Nope. It's a new release, though I can't believe a publisher would still accept something like this."

"So you don't stock it in your store?" I asked. Ginny was the manager of a bookstore up in Rochester, a town about twenty minutes away from our house. As a lifelong bookworm, it was the perfect job for her.

Ginny snorted. "Hell no."

"Well, I think maybe you should keep an open mind," Jen said, a glint in her eye. "You never know, you might learn something useful from that book."

I knew she was half kidding, but I glared at her all the same. "Ha ha. Besides, it's not like I'm exactly hurting for dates. So they don't stick around very long, who cares?"

"Yeah, 'cause you're usually the one telling them to get lost," Ginny said.

She had a point. I guess I subscribed to the quantity over quality philosophy when it came to guys. Sure, I liked dating and meeting new people, and I had a special weakness for the sensitive artist type, but I never saw a reason to keep the same guy around for very long. There were so many more new ones out there just waiting for me to get to them.

"Don't you want a real boyfriend?" Jen asked seriously. "I mean, I know you joke around about how useless men are, but wouldn't you want someone a little more permanent in your life?"

"Where's the fun in that?" I asked. When Jen continued to look skeptical, I pointed at her. "Don't *you* ever get bored with the same guy? Every single day, always the same?"

This was a mistake. Jen got that dopey look on her face that she always wore when she talked about her boyfriend, Matt. Admittedly, he was totally hot and quite a catch, but it was still enough to make you gag.

"Look," I said quickly, hoping to head her off before she got too engrossed in whatever Matt-related fantasy was making her eyes go all glazed over like that. "I'm glad you both have permanent guys, if that's what you want. I'm happy that you're happy. But I haven't yet met a man that I could count on. So what's the point in worrying about it?"

Out of the corner of my eye, I saw Ginny give me a meaningful look, which I ignored. "Look, let's drop it, okay? Jen, tell me about work. Any fun parties on the horizon?"

As Jen began to tell us about the next wedding she was planning, I tried to quell the uncomfortable feeling in my stomach. I *wasn't* interested in a more permanent relationship with a guy. I really wasn't.

Unfortunately, I couldn't shake Ginny's knowing glance for the rest of the meal.

Chapter Three

On the following Thursday, I got home from work to find Tina laying stock-still in the living room, flat on her back on the hardwood floor. Her eyes were closed and she was breathing in an exaggerated, even way.

"Hey," I said, not even bothering to ask her what she was doing. Her answer would probably only confuse me anyhow.

"Hello, Annie," she said in her airy-fairy voice. "Please try not to disturb me; I'm very focused right now."

I rolled my eyes silently and proceeded down the hall to my bedroom. I couldn't worry about crazy Tina right now. I had my audition tomorrow and I was way behind in my prep work.

I slipped into some comfortable clothes and turned soft classical music on my computer. Music always helped me to focus and get in a relaxed mood. I pulled my monologue book from my purse and lay flat on my bed, reading through the lines and absorbing as much as I could. Once I felt comfortable with the material, I stood in the middle of my room and tried to block out some movement—nothing major, just a few things to give me focus and help keep me loose.

By then I was feeling pretty good about the entire process. The monologue I had chosen was really good; it let me be funny and emotional in equal measure. Since Jenner's show was brand new, no one really knew what the feel of it would be. It was really important for me to show my range.

Once I had my blocking down, I was feeling pretty immersed in my character. It was a feeling that I loved, the entire reason I forced myself to work so hard, always slogging away at these auditions and going through so much rejection. This feeling of my own personality giving way, the feeling of truly becoming my character is what kept me coming back for more.

I smiled at myself in the mirror, allowing myself a short moment of pride, before hitting it again from the beginning. My plans were disrupted though—at that moment I heard loud, rhythmic chanting in some unrecognizable language coming from the living room. I groaned. Tina was doing something else crazy out there.

I looked over at my clock and was shocked to find that I had been at it for almost two hours. I decided it was time to go get a snack and maybe give my roommate a taste of her own medicine.

I sauntered into the kitchen, completely ignoring whatever she was doing in the living room. Instead I started loudly singing Britney Spears to myself—it was the most annoying thing I could think of. I heard the chanting pause, and then stop altogether, and I grinned as I pulled a bag of potato chips down from the top shelf.

"Excuse me," Tina said, appearing in the doorway. She was dressed in her normal get-up of black leggings and a flowing tunic. Multiple scarves and bangles dangled from her neck. "You're really disturbing the vibes in this house with that garbage."

"What garbage is that, Tina?" I asked innocently.

"The singing," she said, losing her earth child demeanor and allowing her irritation to show through.

I grinned again. I loved it when her fake hippie persona cracked.

"Sorry about that," I said. "But while we're on the subject, did you ever think that your chanting might be disturbing *me*? I have a really big audition tomorrow."

"My chanting benefits everyone in this house," Tina said, her misty voice returning. "Seriously, Annie, I would think that you would thank me. I improve the aura of this house tremendously. Ugh, if you could only see what it looked like when I moved in here."

I rolled my eyes. "It looked a lot cleaner before you moved in here," I said, gesturing around the kitchen that was now cluttered with dishes, though it had been spotless before Jen and I left for work. "Is picking up after yourself too mundane for someone with your abilities for aura cleansing?"

She glared at me. "You just have no respect for the vibrations that I effect on a daily basis. It's sad really. For a supposed artist you are very closed-minded."

"What can I say, Tina? You're one of a kind." I struggled to control my temper. "Regardless, I have a lot of work to do, and I would really appreciate it if you kept it down. Or, you know, left. That would work for me, too."

She turned around and stomped off so quickly that her scarves billowed out behind her. I sighed. Jen would be mad at me if she knew I had been so mean to Tina. We did need her for rent.

Ever since Ginny had married Josh and moved out, it'd been tough for us to make ends meet. Jen quitting her job at a high-end event-planning firm in order to open up shop with her friend Kiki hadn't helped our situation much—not that I was complaining about that. Jen was so much happier now that she was working with Kiki.

I brought my chips and a pop out to the now vacated living room and sat down on the couch, wondering when Jen was going to be home. When she had worked at her old firm, I would know not to expect her before dinner most nights. She worked herself sick there, always trying to get ahead and prove herself. When Kiki's family hired the firm to plan her mega-platinum wedding, I was worried Jen might actually have a breakdown. As it was, she got totally overwhelmed and almost completely ruined Ginny and Josh's wedding in the process.

I know she still felt terrible about it, even though she had managed to salvage the event at the last minute. When she told us she was quitting her job and starting up with Kiki, who had become a good friend during the wedding planning process, it felt like I was getting my old friend back. So far, things had been going okay for them, no doubt helped along by the fact that Kiki was totally loaded and knew a lot of other rich people in desperate need of help in throwing parties.

I finished off my chips and stood up, stretching. There was no sound coming from Tina's bedroom upstairs. Maybe she had taken my advice and left after all. I figured I may as well use the peace and quiet to make some headway on my monologue.

I was going to nail this audition if it killed me.

Chapter Four

'Are you a working girl? The office can be a great place to meet your dream guy! You spend most of your day at work, so to discount it as a man-meeting opportunity would be foolish. Plus, if you are privy to a man's work habits you'll be able to determine how likely he is to be a good provider! While it might be tempting to neglect your early morning toilette when in a rush to get to work, I can't stress enough the importance of always looking your best. You never know when you might meet Mr. Right!' —**The Single Girl's Guide to Finding True Love**

"Sandra, put that *down*."

"But I want mine to be pink!" the eight-year-old beside me whined, her hand once again drifting toward the bottle of hot pink dye.

"I don't care," I said, reaching forward to move the bottle out of her grasp. "We're doing one color at a time. I've told you that. Several times."

"Fine," she pouted, grabbing her bottle of blue dye and squeezing liberally all over the t-shirt in front of her.

I turned my attention back to Justin, who was making a terrible mess out of his tye-dye project. "Buddy," I told him. "I think that's enough green. Maybe go for something lighter."

Justin looked up at me and grinned, showing that he had somehow managed to get dye all over his face, despite my best efforts to keep the kids well-covered in smocks and gloves. I sighed. "Better get you into the bathroom," I told him, gingerly taking his hand.

"Chris?" I called down the table to my co-worker. He looked up at me and I had to laugh. He looked sweaty and irritated and totally not into the fact that he was spending his Saturday morning helping the kids in the theater camp tye-dye. "I'm taking Justin inside. Keep an eye on Sandra, okay?" I looked down at the little girl, whose hand was once again reaching for the pink dye. "She's having a bit of trouble listening," I said, an edge to my voice. She looked up at me and smiled sheepishly. It was a good thing she was so cute—otherwise Sandra would annoy the crap out of me.

I took Justin back inside the theater, sighing in relief at the cool air. I steered him over to the boys bathroom and set him up at the sink with soap. "Scrub your hands and face, okay?"

I walked back out into the theater lobby and collapsed into a chair. I was exhausted. My audition for Jenner Collins' show had been the night before. To be honest, I think I nailed it. I don't like to brag, but I felt really, really good about that audition. To celebrate, Ginny and Josh had taken me out for dinner, where I had enjoyed a few too many vodka cranberries.

In retrospect, that was a big mistake. Saturday morning theater camp was never an easy task, especially when it was this hot outside, but add a hangover and a killer headache and I was desperately hurting.

"Annie?"

I spun around and saw Grayson, a slightly senior co-worker, standing in the doorway to the stairs. I hadn't realized he'd been up in the office, but I shouldn't be surprised. Though our job titles were nearly identical, Grayson had a tendency to act like he owned this place. It was totally annoying.

"Why are you inside?" he asked. "I thought you were running camp."

I tamped down a flash of irritation. Grayson always talked to me this way; like he was constantly judging my intentions. His bossiness got old really fast.

"I had to bring Justin in," I told him, pointing to the bathroom. "He got some dye on his face. Chris and Maureen are still outside with the kids."

He just nodded as she turned to go. "I have some stuff for you to do in the office," He said over his shoulder. "Make sure you stop by after the kids leave."

Once he was gone, I swore under my breath. I was not scheduled for office hours today. Why did he always assume I would just be at his disposal? Where did he get off bossing me around in the first place? I didn't get paid enough for this shit.

"All done!" Justin said proudly, appearing in the doorway to the bathroom and holding up his clean hands. I looked at him closely. I could definitely make out a few smudges of green around his mouth, but I guess it was better than nothing. "Alright, buddy," I sighed, taking his hand again. "Let's go see what mess Sandra has made in the last five minutes."

***

Two hours later I collapsed in my desk chair. The kids had finally all left, though several of the parents had, of course, been late. Most of the kids in our program were from this neighborhood, which meant that most of them came from single-parent homes. Most days, I was just happy that their parents could get them here at all.

I looked down at the pile of crap Grayson had left for me to finish before he left. He wanted me to work on a program proposal for the local high schools. Great. Just what I felt like doing.

Before I could get started, my cell phone rang. I looked at the screen and groaned. My mother.

"Hey, Mom," I said, closing my eyes.

"Hello, Annie, dear," my mother said. "How are you?"

"I'm good," I told her. "How are you?"

"Oh, fine, fine," she said. "I just finished my afghan, you know the one I was knitting for Beth? It turned out just lovely, very warm and cozy. I was thinking I would start on yours next, dear; it would be just the thing for you and Jen in that drafty old house."

"I have plenty of blankets, Mom," I told her, rubbing my throbbing temple. "And our house isn't that old."

"Well, if you're sure, dear," she said, sounding doubtful. "But I'd be happy to make you one if you change your mind."

"Okay, Mom," I said, trying to tamp down my irritation. Had she really called me just to talk about afghans?

"So what are you up to today?" she asked.

"I'm still at work," I told her. "I had a few things to do after camp was over."

"Are you sure you aren't working too hard?" she asked. "It seems like every time I talk to you you're either at work or running around with the girls. Won't you wear yourself down this way?"

"I'm fine," I said, struggling to keep from snapping at her. My mother was so annoying.

"Well, I just don't know how any of your friends have met their young gentlemen when the three of you are always so busy," she said.

I sighed. Here we went again. If I ever had a conversation with my mother that didn't end up being about my lack of boyfriend, I might just drop dead from shock.

"It's a mystery of modern society," I muttered.

"Well, it just surprises me is all," she said. "Dear, did you happen to get that book I sent you last week? I was worried because I hadn't heard from you about it..."

"I got it, Mom," I said. "I didn't call because I assumed it was a joke."

"Why would it be a joke?" she asked.

"Because I thought you would know, after countless conversations on the subject, that I'm in no hurry to get a boyfriend. I'm very happy with my friends and my life and the men that I date and I don't see any reason for any of that to change now, or any time in the near future. Does that make it clear enough?"

On the other end of the phone, my mother sniffed. "I just don't understand why you don't want a nice man in your life. I know you say you're happy, but what girl doesn't want to get married?"

Because that worked out so well for you, I thought angrily.

"Mom," I said, breathing heavily. "Please, please drop it, okay? I am perfectly happy. I don't need dating tips from some book. Okay?"

"But doesn't it ever bother you that Ginny and Jen are both so happy with their gentlemen, and you're...you're..."

"All by myself?" I asked. "Turning into an old maid? Becoming a spinster?"

"There is no reason for you to take that tone of voice with me," she said, sounding wounded. "I just worry. I'm your mother."

"*I'm fine.*"

"Well, dear, I suppose we should just change the subject then," she said, clearly deeply offended. "How is Danny doing? Do you think *he* might like a new blanket?"

I closed my eyes again and settled into my chair, resigned to the fact that I wouldn't be getting her off the phone any time soon. As she rattled on about the pattern she thought she might use, I looked down at the pile of work on my desk. It was only two p.m., but I had a feeling it was going to be a long, long afternoon.

***

When I got home that evening, I was pleased to see Jen's car in the drive. I hoped that Matt wouldn't be there. I liked him very much and I thought he was totally perfect for Jen, but I wasn't quite in the mood to share my best friend tonight.

Before I could even get to the top of the steps, Kiki was throwing the front door open. "Annie!" she cried. "I'm so, so happy you're here!"

"Hey, Kiki," I said, fighting my disappointment. She was a lot to take, Kiki, but once you warmed up to her she wasn't so bad. After the day I'd had, though, I wasn't sure how much of her I could handle.

"I came over so we could talk about the event," she said, moving over so I could squeeze past her through the doorway. "We have, like, so much work to do."

"Crap," I muttered, dropping my purse on the coffee table. "I totally forgot."

Jen and Kiki had agreed to plan a fundraising benefit for the theater in the following month. It was really generous of them, as we wouldn't be able to pay them much at all, but Jen assured me they would benefit from the goodwill publicity. Their firm was very new and could use all the positive PR they could get.

"Well," Kiki said, following me into the kitchen. "I have some news for you. And it's gonna make you totally happy, I promise."

"Great, Kiks," I told her, grabbing the water pitcher from the fridge. "So...uh, is Jen here?"

"I'm back here," Jen called from her bedroom. "I'll be right out!"

Kiki followed me back to the living room, kind of like a little puppy, and we both sat on the couch.

"So Jen told me you had an audition this week," she said. "That is, like, so cool. For Jenner Collins? Oh my God, I just love him so much. Daddy has done some work with him. He's totally into the revitalization of the city. It's so, so awesome."

"Yup," I agreed, putting my feet up on the coffee table. "He's a pretty cool guy."

"So was he there? At the audition, I mean. How did it go? I bet you were just great."

Kiki always talked like this, a mile a minute. When I first met her I had thought she was the most ridiculous person in the world. But I soon came to find out that she was genuinely this nice, this interested in other people. There was nothing fake about her enthusiasm. She was a good person to have on your side.

"Jenner wasn't there, no" I told her. "It was only the first audition. I wouldn't imagine he'd be around until the callback, if then. For all I know he won't even have much to do with this show; he might just be producing in name only."

"Well, I bet you get the part. And I'm sure he'll be around for at least the performances. He'll probably be, like, so impressed with you."

"Thanks, Kiki," I said, smiling in spite of myself. "So, what's this awesome news about the event?"

"I actually have two awesome pieces of news," she said, bouncing on the couch a little. "But I can only tell you one part right now. The rest will have to wait."

"Um...okay?" I said, wishing I could just go lay down in my quiet room. My headache was coming back with a vengeance.

"Jen," Kiki called. "Hurry up and get out here! I want to tell Annie the news!"

"I'm here," Jen said, appearing in the hallway. "Hey, Ann," she said, shooting me an understanding smile. "How are you feeling?"

"Pretty rough," I admitted.

"What's wrong?" Kiki asked.

"Was just out late last night," I explained. "A little hung over."

"Oh, you poor thing! And here I was talking your ear off when you probably only wanted some piece and quiet. I'm, like, so sorry. But I promise, this news will cheer you up!"

"Okay, Kiki," I told her. "Shoot."

"So, I told Daddy about this event Jen and I are helping you with. And he was totally curious about your organization. He hasn't done too much work out in that neighborhood, you know?"

I nodded, trying to keep up. Kiki's dad, Jonathon Barker, was one of the most well-known and prestigious developers in the city. He had made a ridiculous amount of money revitalizing run-down buildings and neighborhoods in Detroit. He was now the owner of numerous restaurants, clubs and hotels in the city, but to my knowledge his business hadn't ventured much into the area where my theater was located.

"So, anyhow," she said. "I had Jen talk to him and tell him about what you guys do, and he was totally into it. He wants to give the theater some money! Like, not a crazy amount, but he wants to be a patron. And as he gets to know you guys more, who knows how far the relationship will go, you know? My dad is all about building relationships."

I stared at her blankly. What was she saying?

"He's going to become a donor, Annie," Jen explained, smiling broadly at me. "He wants to come out to the benefit next month and get set up as a patron."

"Oh my God," I said, looking between the two of them. "Are you serious?"

Kiki just beamed at me. "See? I told you it would cheer you up!"

"This is...wow, this is just incredible!" I tried to wrap my mind around what Kiki was saying. Springwells was a pretty small theater, even amongst non-profits. We were constantly struggling to come up with funding. If we actually got a patron, especially someone at the level of Jonathon Barker...it could totally change everything.

"He wants to meet with you next week," she said, still smiling. "Nothing formal, just a lunch."

"Wow," I said. "Kiki this is...well, thanks. This is amazing."

"I did nothing," she said, holding up her hands. "This isn't a favor. I just mentioned the event. He was genuinely impressed with what you guys do for the community."

"Wow," I said again, shaking my head.

"So, what's the other news?" Jen asked hopefully, but Kiki just laughed.

"Nope, I told you you'd have to wait." Kiki said.

"You don't know, either?" I asked.

Jen shook her head. "Kiki said we're waiting for everyone else."

"Everyone else?" I asked. "Like, who?"

Just then the front door banged open, revealing Ginny, Josh, and Danny.

"Yay!" Kiki squealed. "I'm so glad you guys are here!"

"Hi," Ginny said, plopping Danny's diaper bag on the floor. "So what's this big news?"

"We're just waiting for Matty and Eric now," Kiki said happily.

"How are you doing today, Ann?" Josh asked, smirking at me. "You were pretty far gone last night."

I rolled my eyes at him. "I feel great," I said. "Just peachy, thanks."

"She should," Jen replied, walking over to grab Danny from Josh's arms. "Kiki just told her Mr. Barker wants to donate to the theater."

"Wow!" Ginny said, coming over to sit down. "That's amazing! Marilyn is gonna totally be thrilled with you!"

"Hmm, I hadn't thought about that," I said. "But she probably will." It was a comforting thought; my boss was a really cool lady, totally dedicated to the theater and our kids. I wished she would see through more of Grayson's kissing up, but I really liked the idea of impressing her myself. Maybe this would give me a shot at getting more of the creative assignments.

There was a loud knock on the door. "Come in!" I hollered. The door opened to reveal Matt and his brother—Kiki's husband, Eric. I rolled my eyes. "Matt, you spend the night here four nights out of week. You don't have to knock on the door."

"I'm trying to be respectful," he said. "For all I know the two of you regularly hang out in your nighties having pillow fights when I'm not around."

Jen snorted. "Like that ever happens."

"Jennifer," he replied, putting his hand over his heart. "Please do not kill my dream."

"Pig," she muttered, but walked over to kiss him hello all the same.

"Okay, Kiki," Matt said, his arm around Jen. "You told me this was an emergency. What's going on?"

"Well, I have really, really awesome news!" she said. "Daddy is working on this deal with a developer to add a hotel to the new casino."

I wrinkled my nose a little bit. I was not really a fan of the Detroit casinos. They depressed the hell out of me, to be honest. Any time I had been inside of one I was overwhelmed by the number of poor people sitting there throwing their money away in the hopes of changing their situation. Detroit had enough problems without adding institutionalized gambling.

"So anyhow, the guy wants Daddy to do a little market research, find out the kind of thing people our age would be looking for in a high class casino hotel.

So Daddy asked me if I wanted to get a group of my friends together and go do some research."

"What do you mean, research?" I asked.

"I mean, the seven of us are going to stay in a swanky hotel!" Kiki said, literally bouncing on the seat now in her excitement.

"Where's there a hotel like that around here?" Matt asked. "That your dad doesn't already own, that is?"

"There isn't," Kiki said, her voice rising in volume with each word. "That's why he wants us to go..." She paused for dramatic effect. We all stared at her. "To Vegas!" she cried.

There was silence in the room for a minute, then Jen let out a little yelp. "We're going to *Vegas?*"

"Yes!" Kiki cried, jumping up from the couch. "The developer got us three rooms at an awesome hotel right on the strip. He wants us to go for a long weekend and come back to tell him all about it. Isn't that amazing?"

I stared at her blankly. It did sound amazing. It also sounded expensive.

"Kiki," I said, feeling uncomfortable. "This is really awesome and everything; a free room sounds great...but I don't think I could afford the airfare or gambling money."

"Don't be silly!" Kiki cried. "Daddy has a jet, you know that. And this is totally for business so I'm allowed to use it. And the hotel will give us comps for the casino. The whole point is for us to have a great time so we can report back to Daddy and his partners what we liked."

"Holy shit," Ginny said. "Are you seriously offering us a totally free trip to Vegas?"

"Yes!" Kiki said, sounding relieved that we were finally catching on. "Well, I'm not. Daddy and his partner are."

I just stared at her for a minute. Vegas. I had never been farther west than Chicago. And then it had only been to visit Jen at college, staying in her cramped little dorm. Nothing at all like what Kiki was offering.

"I can't believe you guys aren't more excited," Kiki said, starting to pout. "Are you worried about the money? That's it, isn't it?" As a wealthy heiress, Kiki had a very hard time understanding why the issue of money so often made the rest of us uncomfortable.

But this...like she said, it wasn't like she or her dad were just giving us a trip to be nice. Business people must do stuff like this all the time, right? I mean, not that I knew too many business people. But weren't they always spending money on this kind of thing?

Jen had gone on Mr. Barker's jet a few times, for work. She said it was the most amazing thing, total luxury and swank. And then we would get to spend the weekend in a suite in Vegas. I could only imagine what kind of place we would be going to. I hadn't been on a trip in so long, and I'd never been anywhere so cool.

I felt a sudden flash of excitement, and before I knew it, I was jumping off the couch to hug Kiki. "This is amazing!" I cried. I saw Jen look at me in surprise. Hugging Kiki and jumping around in excitement weren't really my style. But I didn't care. We were going to Vegas!

"Seriously!" Ginny cried, jumping up too. Danny, seeing her reaction, started clapping. Ginny also wrapped her arms around Kiki, who seemed overjoyed at our reaction.

"Oh my God, we're going to Vegas, baby!" I shouted.

I looked over and saw that even calm, collected Matt was looking excited. He gave his brother Eric a high five and hugged Jen.

"Josh, why the hell aren't you excited?" Ginny asked accusingly. I looked over and saw that Josh was sitting on the couch, a rather disappointed look on his face.

"I won't be able to go," he said softly. "Sorry, Kiki," he added, looking up at her. "But there's just no way I'll be able to get a Saturday off."

Ginny groaned. Josh had recently started a new job at a local magazine. It was the kind of work he'd wanted to do his entire life, literally his dream job. But he had just started a few months ago and was working his way up from the bottom. His current assignment was to cover weekend events all over the metro area. Saturdays were always his busy day.

"I just haven't been there long enough to get the time off," he said. "I'm really sorry."

Ginny looked like she was going to cry. "That's okay," she said. "I'm sure there will be other trips. You guys will just have to tell me all about it."

"Are you crazy?" Josh asked, staring at her. "Why on earth shouldn't you go with them?"

"I can't just leave you here to work while I go on vacation!" she said.

"Oh, yes you can, and you will. No way are you missing out on something this cool just because of me."

"Josh..." she started.

"Seriously, Gin," he said firmly. "You're going. I'll stay home with my little Danny bud here and we'll have a man's weekend. We'll smoke cigars and watch racy movies and walk around in our underwear. It will be a blast."

I felt a rush of affection for Ginny's husband. They may have gotten off to a rocky start, but I loved him for wanting this for her, for trying to convince her it was nothing rather than act like some kind of martyr.

I looked at Ginny and realized it wouldn't take too much to convince her. She clearly wanted to go, bad.

"Gin," I told her. "I'm gonna need a roommate. Please come with us and bunk with me so I don't end up having to sleep in a rollaway bed in Jen and Matt's room. Please."

She laughed, then turned to her husband. "Josh, are you *sure* you don't care?"

"Absolutely," he said. "And who knows, maybe you'll strike it big at blackjack and we'll be rolling in the dough by the time you come home."

"So when is this?" Matt asked.

"That's the best part. It's next weekend! We're leaving Thursday—we don't even have to wait that long." She took a deep breath. "And I think I would seriously die if we had to wait. Not being able to tell Jen all day has been *killing* me."

I was so excited, I managed to not even roll my eyes at that.

My phone rang, distracting me from the excited plans everyone had started to make. I looked at the screen and didn't recognize the number. "Probably a bill collector," I muttered, but was still too excited to care. I headed to the hallway for a little more quiet before answering.

"Hello?" I asked.

"Miss Duncan?" said an unfamiliar male voice. Definitely a bill collector.

"Yes?"

"This is Jackson Coles, from the JCollins Theater team." I managed to stifle my gasp. This was the man I had read for the night before.

"We were very impressed with your audition last night," Jackson continued, and I felt my heart start to beat rapidly in my chest.

"We would be pleased to offer you a place at our callbacks this week."

"Wow," I stammered, feeling totally shocked. I couldn't believe they were getting back to me already. And I really couldn't believe they wanted to see me again. "That sounds great. I would be very interested in attending."

"Great," Jackson said. "Let me give you the details." He read out a date and location and instructed me on where to find the audition materials online. "We'd like you to read for the part of Jillian," he said, and I felt like passing out. That was the largest female role.

"That sounds great," I said, barely recognizing my own voice. I felt my hands shaking and I prayed I wouldn't say anything stupid to give myself away.

"So we'll see you on Wednesday evening," he confirmed.

"Absolutely," I said. "Thank you so much."

I hung up the phone and stared at the wall blankly. I could hardly believe that only a few hours ago I was cursing Grayson and my mother and feeling so frustrated with everything. Within the space of an afternoon I had found out about a possible sponsor to the theater, the trip to Vegas, and now this.

I walked slowly back to the living room and watched my friends for a moment. Jen was sitting close to Matt, holding his hand while they excitedly talked about the trip. Ginny was bouncing Danny on her lap while Josh sat at her feet. They all looked happy, excited.

I've been jealous, I realized suddenly. I never would have thought it of myself. I loved my friends more than anything else in the world. I wanted their happiness as much as my own. But deep down inside I'd been jealous that they were settled, that they were successful, that they knew what they wanted and were on their way to getting it.

Now, for the first time, I realized I just might be, too.

Chapter Five

*'Do you feel nervous when conversing with the opposite sex? It's a very normal response for many young ladies, and nothing to worry about. If you take the process of finding a mate seriously, then it's natural you'd have some nerves when you meet the potential Mr. Right. Instead of dwelling on this, do your best to act confident. There are few things more appealing to a man than a woman who is sure of herself.'—**The Single Girl's Guide to Finding True Love**

I felt a healthy dose of fear as the callback approached. I tried to tell myself that it was pointless to get worked up about it. Whatever happened would happen and the best thing I could do to help myself was stay loose and try not to feel anxious. Stress would only make my performance worse so it was essential I stay calm.

I told myself that, but it was really hard to actually *do*.

"This could be it," I told Jen the night before the callback. She had been running lines with me for the past two hours and I now felt that I was as ready as I was going to get. "I mean, this could be my big break."

"You can't think about it that way," Jen told me firmly. "Seriously, Ann. If you let yourself even think about 'big breaks' and all of that, you're going to freak

34

out. Just treat it like any other audition. I mean, how many of these have you done?"

"Dozens," I told her, thinking back to all the seemingly endless (and mostly fruitless) auditions I had been on since I first picked up the acting bug in high school.

"You have to convince yourself it's just like all the rest," she told me. "You're prepared, you know your stuff. If you can go in there with a confident attitude and just relax, I think you'll do really, really well."

She was right. She usually was. But it was much harder to actually act on.

I pulled up in front of a small theater on the outskirts of the city. I had seen a few live bands here over the years, and somehow I felt comforted by the familiar setting.

This is your turf, I reminded myself. *You've been working in this city for years now. There's nothing to worry about.*

I entered the building, trying to tamp down the nerves. A sign in the lobby directed me through to the stage area. I could make out a clump of people down by the stage and I headed in their direction.

A skinny man met me in the aisle. I recognized him as Jackson Coles, the man I had read for in my initial audition. He looked busy and impatient and I was very relieved that I was early. "Name?" he asked briskly.

"Annie Duncan," I said, burying my hands in my pockets to stop them from shaking.

"Good. You'll go in the first group here." He gestured behind him to the small group of people waiting by the stage. "We're just waiting for one more."

The man handed me a stack of stapled papers before turning away to talk quietly with the woman sitting next to him.

Well, at least they're welcoming, I thought to myself sarcastically. I took the papers and headed toward my group.

"Hi," said a girl who looked to be a few years younger than me. She was gorgeous, totally perfect. She had porcelain white skin and long, silky blond hair. I felt intimated by her immediately, though she was smiling kindly at me.

"Are you as nervous as me?" she asked.

I smiled back. "Yeah, pretty nervous."

"This is my first audition," she continued, leaning toward me conspiratorially. Great. She had managed to pull a major callback on her first try. Brat.

"Do you think he'll be here?" she asked.

"Who?"

"Jenner Collins!" she replied, looking surprised that I hadn't known immediately. "I mean, it is his show, you know? I heard a rumor he plans to actually *direct* the show. Don't you think he would want to be involved in the casting?"

"I bet he's pretty busy," I said, shrugging. I didn't need to be worrying about Collins in addition to all the nerves I was already battling.

"Oh, wouldn't you just die if he was here?" the girl continued, closing her eyes while a dreamy smile lit up her face. I rolled my eyes. "He's just so gorgeous and successful. I would love to meet him."

I found myself feeling a little better as Jackson called for us to head to the stage. I may not be as heartbreakingly beautiful, or as young, or as lucky, as the blond girl—but at least I had a bit better sense than to get all star-struck like that.

"Okay, listen up," Jackson called out. "We're going to start with some cold readings. We'd like everyone to stand out to the side until we call your name. We might have you read in some odd pairings and we might want to see you in different roles than you prepared for. We ask you please to just go for it and do your best. We're looking to see how flexible you can be, how quick you are on your toes. We'll be asking for some more in-depth character readings a little later."

I was relieved not to be one of the first ones called. The lights on the stage were very bright and the theater seemed to stretch out endlessly behind the seats where Jackson and his partner had set up. I was feeling those nerves return and I was grateful for the moment's reprieve to gather my thoughts—and check out the competition a little, of course.

The first three actors they called forward were clearly good. The two men carried themselves with that confident air that only comes with true comfortableness. The girl that had read first seemed thrown by the activity. She had been asked to read for an older woman, though she appeared to be no more than twenty-five. I suspected that she had studied her lines ad nauseam last night and she didn't seem to be adapting well to having to read something unfamiliar.

When it was my turn, I was asked to read one of the male parts. Determined not to let it throw me, I made sure to read clearly and loudly. At one point during the reading, I thought I saw another figure join the two in the back, but I was concentrating so much on the unfamiliar lines that I didn't let it phase me.

The readings went on like that for some time. I was asked to read several more times and I soon noticed that I had read with every combination of males on the stage. In fact, it started to feel like I was being called forward more often than any of the other girls. I wondered if that was a good sign.

"Okay, thank you!" Jackson called out finally. "That gave us a chance to see you all paired up together. Now we want to see you do a bit of improv."

Yes, I thought to myself. I loved improv. And I was pretty darn good at it, if I do say so myself. There was a group of people that I knew from college who would occasionally hang out at a local comedy club on open mic nights to do improv sets—kind of like karaoke for actors. I enjoyed meeting up with them and having a go at it. Something about the way you had to just jump in—there was no room for anything cerebral, no room for any self doubt. You either did it, or you didn't. It was a very freeing feeling.

Jackson directed us all to sit in the front row while he called groups up one at a time to participate. I was a little bummed when I wasn't called first. That's when it hit me—I was barely nervous anymore! I had, once again, lost myself in the act of performing. It was a good feeling. It made me think that maybe I belonged here.

"I can't believe he's here!" the blond girl whispered to me as the first group took the stage. "I mean, I knew he might show up, but to actually see him back there, not even fifteen feet away!"

"What are you talking about?" I whispered back, wishing she would shut up so I could concentrate on the scene on stage.

"Jenner Collins!" the blond girl hissed quietly in my ear. "He walked in while we were reading. Did you see him?"

I had actually forgotten all about Jenner Collins. He must have been the figure that I thought I saw enter during my reading. I was determined not to think about it at all.

"I'd rather focus on the exercise," I told her, my voice flat. I hoped that she would take the hint that I wasn't in the mood to talk to her about this.

Unfortunately, she didn't. For the entire first exercise she kept up a running commentary about how much she loved Collins, what a great actor he was, how inspiring it was to be in the same room with him, let alone perform for him.

Her constant gushing did nothing to change my frame of mind. In fact, it made me feel so irritated that I was soon projecting that on Jenner himself. Who the hell did he think he was anyhow? Some useless Hollywood pretty boy. Whatever. Why would I let myself get worked up over him?

Looking back on it, I should probably thank blond girl for annoying me so much. When they finally called my name to participate in an exercise, I was feeling completely confident—cocky almost—and not at all star struck.

There were a few who couldn't say the same. The same younger woman I had noticed in the first reading was placed in my group. Throughout the exercise she kept looking nervously out into the audience. She missed a few opportunities to add an obvious line. *Oh well*, I thought to myself. Her problem. If she wanted to be all star struck by Collins, she could go right ahead. I had more important things to do.

The improv exercise felt great. They asked us to play a game called Dinner Party. One participant played the party host, while the rest of us were assigned silly mystery characters. The host then had to guess who we were based on our lines and behavior. I was given a piece of paper with the name Monica

Lewinsky on it. I quickly decided to let go and have fun with it. I was highly gratified to hear some laughter in the darkness as I continually tried to rub an imaginary stain off the leg of my jeans.

After everyone had a chance to participate in an exercise, they finally called us up in pairs to read our prepared lines. This time I was called first. I was paired with a handsome older guy with slightly graying hair. In the scene, he was playing my father while I played Jillian, a young woman struggling to overcome the abuse she had faced in her childhood.

From my preparations with Jen the night before, I had already fallen in love with this character. She was a lot like me, to be honest. A little bit sarcastic, a little on the dry side. But underneath her tough exterior you could tell she was very passionate, very loyal. Jen too had told me that the character reminded her of me. I took it as a compliment.

I felt good during the reading. The guy I was reading with was clearly talented, and we fell into a rhythm with each other quickly. When Jackson called time on us, I actually felt disappointed. I would have liked to keep going.

I didn't have to wait long. I was called back up several more times. I read with two more older men, both reading the role of Jillian's father. I was then asked to read with two different young guys. One, a tall, thin guy about my age, was really cute. I could feel a chemistry bouncing between us from the first few lines. It's such a funny thing, how strong that indefinable force can be. But I could tell he felt it too, and it made my own reading stronger.

After that, Jackson asked us to hold tight for a minute. We could hear muffled conversation from behind us. I assumed he was talking to his partner and to Jenner Collins. For the first time since I had started reading, I began to feel nervous.

"Okay, we want to thank you all for coming in," Jackson said, moving up the aisle to stand before us. "We're going to send most of you home now, but there are a few of you that we need to see a little more from."

My heart started pounding at a rapid pace. What did that mean? Was this a nice way of saying that they were making a cut right now? If you were asked to stay, was that a good thing? Or were they sending home the ones they were already sure about?

Jackson started rattling off a list of names. Mine wasn't on it. I felt my palms start sweating. "If I called your name, you can go now. Thank you very much for coming in and we'll be in contact with you early next week."

Oh my God. So that meant they wanted me to stay. I still didn't know if that was a good thing or not, but I hoped it meant they liked me.

Blond girl was *not* asked to stay. She was looking at the ground with a blank expression on her face, and I had a feeling she was fighting tears. She must think being asked to go was a bad sign. In her case, I had to agree. Though she was beautiful, I hadn't felt very much talent in her readings. Maybe she was too worked up about Jenner.

Once the theater had cleared out, Jackson passed out more packets. He told us we would have a few minutes to look over the new material before we started again. When he handed me mine he asked me to look at the part of Kate .

Hmm, so they weren't asking me to continue reading for Jillian. Again, I had no idea how to take this.

When I was called up, I did my best with the new material. It was much harder than it had been reading the lines I had prepared with Jen, but I think I got through it okay. I was again asked to read with the dark haired guy who I had felt such a connection with. This time I managed to catch his name, Tyler, and I think our second reading was as good as our first.

When we had exhausted every possible pairing, Jackson once again asked us to sit while the three of them conferred in the back. This time, I sat next to Tyler. He seemed not at all concerned with the events taking place behind us. Instead of making small talk, he pulled out a phone and began texting. I had to admit, it was a relief over blond girl's incessant chattering.

"Ladies and gentlemen, thank you so much for coming," an unfamiliar voice said. I looked around to see a taller man walking down the aisle toward us, Jackson scurrying behind in his wake.

Oh my God, I thought. It was him.

All of my swagger about not caring about Jenner Collins left my body faster than you could say Golden Globe. I had always thought that he was good-looking in his films and appearances, but up close and in person, Jenner Collins was gorgeous. There was no other word for it.

"We're going to end this for tonight. You've made our decision very difficult," Jenner said, smiling kindly at us. "I would expect to be in contact with all of you early next week," he continued. "Thank you again for participating tonight. I really do appreciate it."

There was a finality in Jenner's words and everyone began to rise from their seats, gathering their things. It all felt very anti-climatic to me. Of course, I hadn't expected to find out my fate tonight, but I didn't much like the idea of having to wait until next week to hear who had succeeded. Why would it take them so long to make their decision? Were they seeing other actors besides us?

Feeling unsettled, I gathered up my things and followed the group out of the theater. No one spoke to me at all as I passed through the lobby. I got to my car, feeling strangely lonely and very scared. No sooner had I started the engine than my phone began to buzz in my pocket. I had turned off the sound while in the audition. Looking at the display I noticed that I had four missed calls. Two from Jen, two from Ginny.

Smiling slightly, I called the house. Jen picked up on the second ring. "We're dying!" she shouted into the phone. "That was the longest audition ever! How did it go?"

I sighed, then put my car in gear, eager to get home to my friends. "To be honest with you," I said, "I have no idea."

Chapter Six

"This is amazing," I said, staring out the window of the limo.

"Yup, pretty much," Ginny agreed, though without the same level of enthusiasm.

I guess I couldn't blame her—I'd been saying basically the same thing all afternoon. But how could you blame me? So far that day I'd been chauffeured to the airport in a limo, flown on a private jet to Las Vegas, where we were picked up at the airport by *another* limo, and now we were zipping down the strip in total luxury while we drank champagne.

I could get used to this kind of life.

"You're totally right, Annie," Kiki said happily, peering out the window at the bright lights. "This is going to be, like, the best weekend ever."

I didn't even roll my eyes at Kiki's words. After a few hours with her, I barely noticed her excessive language. Besides, today my excitement might actually match hers for once.

I looked out the window at the sights of the strip. I had thought downtown Detroit was pretty bright with everything all lit up, but we had *nothing* on Vegas. It was flashing neon as far as the eye could see.

"It looks like our hotel is pretty close to a lot of cool sites," Jen said, looking down at her Vegas guidebook. "We should really make a list of everything we want to see and do, so that we don't miss anything. I mean, we only have three days!"

While Jen's eyes were glued to her guidebook, I rolled my eyes at Ginny. It was so typical of Jen to spend her time researching and planning while the bright lights of Vegas passed her by.

"Oh my God!" Kiki squealed suddenly, and everyone quickly turned to face her.

"What's wrong?" Ginny asked.

"I think we're almost there!" Kiki cried.

Out of the corner of my eye I saw Matt roll his eyes and turn his attention back to the newspaper he was reading. I caught Jen's eye and we broke out into grins. As an old friend and her current brother-in-law, Matt had a lot of experience dealing with the overwhelming force that was Kiki.

"Oooh, we are, we are!" Kiki cried, and I turned my attention back to the window to get a glimpse of our hotel.

"Wow," I whispered, staring up at the massive building in front of us. "It's huge."

"It is," Ginny said next to me, sounding pretty awestruck herself. "And look at all the lights...all the people walking around."

I turned and met her gaze, and saw my own excitement mirrored there. "I think you were right," she said, smiling. "This *is* going to be awesome."

"Come on," Kiki said, literally clapping her hands. "Let's get inside!"

It felt unnatural to me to jump out of the car and leave our luggage behind for someone else to take care of, but I tried to follow Kiki's lead and play it cool.

Once we reached the lobby, however, all pretense of cool went out the window. I couldn't help but gaze around the opulent room with my mouth open. I had never seen anything like it.

"Holy shit," I muttered.

"You said it," Ginny agreed.

Tasteful colored lights reflected off the dark floors and marble columns. Beyond the check-in area I could see giant crystal columns flanking an escalator, all bathed in a soft purple glow. None of it was quite what I expected—definitely not flashy or gaudy. Instead, it struck me as very chic, very cool.

"This says there's a mall in here somewhere," Jen said, turning her attention back to her guidebook as Kiki and Eric headed over to the desk to check us in. "It's supposed to have awesome shopping. And I guess the casino is that way. Oooh, and it says there's a really good club over there..."

"Sweetie," Matt said, taking her hand. "You're on vacation. Let's put the book away and relax, okay?"

"Yeah," Ginny agreed, snatching the book out of her hand. "No planning on this trip. We're all just gonna go with the flow and have fun."

I laughed at the crestfallen expression on Jen's face. For her, planning *was* fun. But letting go a little definitely wouldn't hurt.

"We're all set!" Kiki said, hurrying over to us. "They have us in three different rooms, but they're all really close to each other. And they're supposed to have amazing views."

"Let's go check it out!" I said, feeling like I might soon join Kiki in bouncing around.

As we headed to the elevators, I put my arm through Ginny's. "So," I said. "Are you totally bummed you're stuck rooming with me?"

Gin snorted. "Yeah, right. We're gonna have a blast. It will be like old times."

"Yeah, but won't you miss Josh?"

"Sure. But I'm not going to let it ruin my trip."

"This is why I love you," I told her, as we followed the rest of the group onto the elevator. "You might be an old married fart but you can still have fun without your hubs."

"I'm actually looking forward to it," she said, squeezing my arm a little. "I don't get to see you as often as I want these days."

"We're all gonna have so much fun!" Kiki said, peering around Eric to look at us. "Just you guys wait!"

The elevator pinged as we reached our floor, and I felt another little jolt of excitement. I wondered what the rooms would be like in a place this nice.

"Okay, this is you guys," Eric said, stopping at a door and handing me a small envelope with our key cards. "Jen and Matt, you're two doors down." He handed Matt their cards. "And Kiki and I are right next to them."

The girls and I grinned at each other goofily for a minute, like little kids at Christmas, before we all dived for our doors. I frantically fumbled with the key card, finally getting the door open so Ginny and I could rush inside.

"Wow," Ginny said, stopping in the foyer. "I mean...wow."

I was having trouble finding words. The room was huge, bigger than Jen's and my entire living room. Probably our entire first floor combined. "Did you know she was getting us a suite?" I asked.

"Nope," Ginny said, setting her purse on a small coffee table. "But I sure as hell ain't complaining."

In addition to two queen-sized beds, there was also a living room area and giant floor-to-ceiling windows. The staff had pulled the curtains, giving us a spectacular view of the Vegas strip far below us. I walked over to the window, staring down in amazement.

"You have to see this," I called to Ginny, who had wandered into the bathroom. "There's a replica of the Eiffel tower down there!"

"Hang on," Ginny called. "This bathroom is incredible."

I ran in to check it out and saw Ginny sitting, fully clothed, in the marble tub, testing its size. "This is bigger than our kitchen!" she cried.

I started laughing and found I couldn't stop. I felt giddy with excitement. Ginny started laughing too. "Can you even believe this?" she asked.

"Come look at the view," I told her, grabbing her hand to pull her out of the tub.

We ran back into the living area and stood at the window, gazing down at the lights.

"Oh my God!" Ginny squealed, grabbing my arm and pointing. "It's that fountain! You know, from the George Clooney movie!"

"You're right!" I told her, following her pointing finger down to the Bellagio fountain, which looked familiar to me from *Ocean's Eleven*.

"You guys," a voice said behind us, and we spun around. Jen was standing in the still open doorway. "Isn't this amazing?"

"Do you have a view like this?" Ginny asked.

"Yes!" Jen said, coming over to stand with us. "It's totally incredible!"

"Look at our bathroom!" Ginny said.

"Mine is like that too!" Jen said, sounding more and more like Kiki with every word.

We were saved the embarrassment of jumping around like five-year-olds when the porters showed up with our luggage. Seeing them standing there in the doorway with my bags had the effect of reminding me that I was actually a grown woman. I tipped the porter generously and Jen slipped away to help Matt unpack.

"Late dinner and drinks in half an hour," she called over her shoulder. We had all eaten on the plane, but that felt like hours ago. We had a full night of partying ahead of us and I was determined to have the energy to go the distance.

Chapter Seven

*'While it's important to have confidence when dealing with men, it's equally important not to be too bold. Men like it when you let them make the first move. A woman who insists on ignoring this fact will have a hard time making a man interested in her.'—**The Single Girl's Guide to Finding True Love***

"Wow," I said again. "I know I keep saying it, but this place is unbelievable!"

"I know!" Ginny squealed, grabbing my arm. "Look at all the people!" Our group was standing at the entrance to the casino. Everywhere I looked I was bombarded with noise, lights, conversation, and people. It was so cool.

"What should we do first?" Jen asked.

"Drinks," I said immediately.

"Obviously," Ginny agreed.

We headed over to the bar and placed our orders while we all gazed around. "I want to try this," Jen said excitedly. "I want to learn how to play cards."

Matt chuckled and put his arm around her. "I have a feeling you'd be pretty amazing at that."

"I want to try the slots first," Ginny said.

In the end we decided that Kiki, Jen, Matt, and Eric would head over to the blackjack tables while Ginny and I gave the slot machines a try. The two of us headed to the loudest, most garish machines we could find and sat down together.

"So, how does this work?" Ginny asked, adjusting her sparkly top. She and I couldn't help but to get a little gussied up before coming downstairs, and I was glad we had done so. I had already spotted several guys I wouldn't mind getting to know a little better.

"I think we just put our coins in here?" I said uncertainly.

We decided to give it a try. Within a few minutes we were each out five bucks.

"Wow," Ginny said. "That wasn't quite as much fun as I thought it would be."

"Let's walk around a little," I said. "Do some people-watching."

We grabbed our drinks and made our way deeper into the casino floor. There was so much to look at it was hard to focus on anything. We ended up gathering with a small crowd around a craps table. There was a man there who seemed to be on some kind of roll. Every time the dealer rolled the dice the people around him would start screaming. He seemed to get free drinks every few minutes.

"What's he made so far?" Ginny asked the middle-aged man next to us.

"Oh, he's up to thirty thousand," the man replied.

"Holy hell!" I said. "Seriously?"

The man smiled.

"So how does this work?" Ginny asked him.

"First time in Vegas?" he asked.

"Yeah," Ginny replied. "First time in a casino, actually."

The man started explaining the rules of craps to Gin, and I felt myself zoning out. I just had never found card or dice games to be all that interesting. The money sounded great, sure, but I couldn't really imagine trying to learn all the intricacies that the man was explaining. I let my eyes wander around the crowded floor. There were groups of people everywhere, gambling, chatting, and drinking. I felt the unmistakable feeling of someone's gaze on me, and I turned.

I found myself staring at a man, probably about my age. He was dressed casually in jeans and a tee shirt. His body looked nice, but it was hard to make out his face under his baseball cap. Then it hit me. He was wearing a Detroit Tigers hat.

"Gin," I hissed. She tilted her head in my direction. "See that guy over there?" I asked. She looked in the direction I was indicating.

"Yeah," she said. "So?"

"Do you think he's from Detroit?" I asked.

She squinted. "Hmm. Could be. But a lot of people wear that hat. It's a cool logo and Eminem made it totally famous."

I thought about that. She had a point. But the guy was still looking at me, and I found my curiosity and interest pique.

"Care if I go over and talk to him?" I asked her.

Ginny rolled her eyes at me. "You're such a tramp," she teased.

"Yeah, yeah," I said. "Seriously though, you okay here for a minute?"

She waved me away and I smiled at her. I headed over in the direction of the guy. He was now breaking away from his friends a little and walking in my direction.

"Hey," I said.

Up close he was definitely good looking. Tall and blond, very clean cut. He reminded me a little bit of

Kiki's husband, Eric. He had that football-player, classic-American look to him. Not necessarily my type, but who cared? A little flirting never hurt anyone.

"I've been watching you for ages," he said, then flushed. "Oops, sorry. That sounded totally creepster, didn't it? I just meant that you look familiar to me. I've been trying to place you."

I had a hard time not rolling my eyes. Real original line.

"I noticed your hat," I told him, pointing up at it. "Are you from Detroit?"

"Yeah," he said eagerly. "Well, Birmingham actually, but close enough."

I did roll my eyes at that. Birmingham was a totally ritzy suburban town—about as far from Detroit as you could get, figuratively speaking.

"What about you?" he asked.

"I live in Ferndale," I explained.

"Wow. That's a small world. Maybe I have seen you around then."

I smiled up at him flirtatiously. "Perhaps," I said. I saw him gulp and felt my heart soar a little. He was totally into me.

"So how long are you in Vegas for?" I asked.

"Just the weekend," he replied. "My buddy is getting married in a few weeks; bachelor party, you know." He gestured to the group of guys behind us. "How about you?"

"The same. Well, minus the bachelor party stuff. So, are you guys just getting wasted and getting a bunch of lap dances?"

He laughed. "Hardly. I mean, we're drinking but I don't think any of us would be too into the stripper thing. I have little sisters and I just couldn't imagine ogling a girl like that."

I looked at him, trying to figure him out. He seemed like a pretty nice guy, but it could always just be an act. I'd seen it before.

"So, what are your plans while you guys are in town?" he asked.

"I think we're gonna do the Stratosphere thrill rides tomorrow," I replied. "You know, the ones on top of that tower? And see the Cirque du Soleil show too. Probably do a lot of dancing, that kind of thing."

"That sounds great," he replied. "It would be cool if I saw you around."

"Yeah," I said, smiling again. I had to admit, faker or not, it was nice that he was so clearly into me. "Well, I should get back to my friend."

I couldn't be sure but I thought I saw his face fall. "Yeah?" he asked.

I gestured over to where Ginny was standing, clearly gawking at us. Poor married girl, she had to live vicariously through me when I chatted up new guys.

"Well, I guess I'll see you around," I said, turning to go.

"Wait!" he called after me. "I don't even know your name."

I kept walking. When I had gotten a few feet away I turned back. "It's Annie," I called out, grinning, then turned back to Ginny.

"Like I said—tramp," she sighed when I reached her.

I grinned at her. "Oh, Gin," I said. "You're just jealous."

***

The next morning I rolled out of bed with a pretty major headache. We had casino-hopped 'til all hours of the morning. As Matt had predicted, Jen had turned out to be a phenomenal card player. She had picked up blackjack fairly quickly, and ended the night four hundred bucks richer. The rest of had occupied ourselves with a lot of drinking.

"Ugh," Ginny groaned from the bed next to me. "I keep forgetting that I'm an old married mother and I shouldn't be doing things like this."

"Gin, baby or not, you're only twenty-five," I told her, rubbing my head.

"Let's go get food," she said. "Bacon is the only cure for a hangover this bad."

"Oh my God," I moaned. "Bacon sounds amazing."

We dragged ourselves out of bed, throwing on yoga pants and tank tops. "You look hot," I told Ginny drily as she pulled her hair up in a messy bun.

"Says the girl who didn't manage to take her make-up off last night," she replied.

We made it downstairs to one of the casino restaurants and found a mouth-watering buffet. Ginny was whimpering next to me as we stared down the long line of food. We had never been the kind of girls to avoid food after heavy drinking—or any other time for that matter. We were of the opinion that the best way to kill a hangover was to stuff it full of greasy junk.

A few minutes later, we had found our way to a table with heaping plates of pancakes, bacon, and eggs. "I need coffee," Ginny moaned. "Where the hell is the coffee?"

"Right over there," a voice said.

We both looked up and I found myself face to face with the guy from the casino last night. Oh, hell. He looked even better in the morning, if that was possible, all bright eyed and rested. I'm sure I looked like crap.

"How you doing this morning, Annie?" he asked, sitting down across the table. "Have fun last night?"

"A little too much," I said, feeling uncomfortable at his nearness in my present state.

"Well," he said, "what happens in Vegas stays in Vegas, right?"

Ginny was watching my reaction to his arrival with a smile on her face that freaked me out a little bit. She knew me too well.

"Hi," she said, pushing her hand into his face. "I'm Ginny, Annie's friend."

"Hello, Ginny, Annie's friend," he replied, smiling. "I'm Nate."

"Nice to meet you, Nate," she said, smiling at me way too obviously. Oh, geez.

"So what are you guys up to today?" Nate asked. "Did you say something about thrill rides?"

"Yeah," Ginny said excitedly. "We're gonna go to the stratosphere tower and do the rides up there."

"That's awesome," Nate said. "I've been trying to convince my buddies to do that, but they're way too chicken."

"You could always come with us," Ginny said.

I kicked her under the table. I could live without her matchmaking. It was one thing to flirt with the guy last night, when I was looking good and feeling pretty tipsy. It was another to invite him to spend the day with us.

Nate was looking at me with a slight smirk on his face. "Thanks, Ginny, but I should probably hang out with my friends today."

I gave a sigh of relief, but it was short-lived.

"Well, before we head over there we're going to spend some time at the pool here at the hotel," Ginny said.

"Cool," Nate said. "I'll totally see you guys there."

He tapped the table twice, then stood up. "Good to see you guys, Ginny, Annie."

"Bye!" Ginny said brightly.

"Bye," I muttered.

After he walked away, I turned on her. "What are you doing?" I asked.

"What? I thought you liked him?"

"I think he's cute," I corrected her. "I never said I *liked* him."

She sighed. "Well the only way to find out if you like a cute guy is to spend some time with him."

"Ginny," I said, "he is so obviously not my type. Flirting with him at the casino is one thing. Hanging out with him all day is totally another."

"Why don't you think he's your type?" she asked, surprised. "He's totally into you. And the way you sauntered over to him last night—I think there's chemistry there."

I sighed.

"I know what you're thinking," Ginny said. "You're thinking he's too together for you, right? You're wishing he would be just a little more emo?"

"I don't like emo guys," I said, offended.

Ginny laughed. "Bullshit. Sensitive artist is just another way to describe emo."

I glared at her. "Gin, he's probably, like, an accountant or something. He lives in *Birmingham*."

She shook her head. "You're such a snob."

"Who's a snob?" Jen asked, sitting down next to me. I looked at her and groaned. While Ginny and I looked like we'd been drinking all night, Jen looked as perfect and put-together as ever. Typical.

"Annie made a love connection and she's in denial," Ginny said.

"Oooh," Jen said, digging into her pancakes. "Who's the guy?"

"It's not a love connection," I said, feeling irritated with both of them. "I met a guy from Detroit at the casino last night. I flirted with him a little bit. End of story."

"Or not," Ginny said, drinking her juice. "He came over here this morning and you can totally tell he's into her. He says he's going to try to find her at the pool."

"Wow, Annie," Jen said. "This sounds pretty serious."

"I have an idea," I said, putting down my fork. "How about you both drop it?"

"She says she doesn't care," Ginny said to Jen, ignoring me, "but how much do you want to bet right now she's thinking about what bikini to wear?"

As they both laughed, I could only glare at them.

I mean, she was totally right, but it was still annoying.

Chapter Eight

"So where's the hottie?" Matt asked, settling down on a lounge chair near me. Jen snickered, and I glared at them both.

"Thanks, Jen," I told her.

"What?" she said. "It's very important to me that your future husband gets along well with my boyfriend. I had to make sure that Matt was welcoming to him."

"Future husband?" Kiki squealed as she and Eric joined us in the area we had staked out by the pool. "Who is it, Annie?"

I groaned. "You guys, seriously. It's no big deal. Please don't embarrass me."

"Because you have never, ever embarrassed either of us around a guy," Ginny said drily. I flipped her off.

"Hey, Nate!" Ginny said suddenly, staring at the space behind my head. I jumped in surprise and I saw Jen snicker out of the corner of my eye.

"Hey, guys," Nate said.

"Annie, why don't you introduce us to your friend?" Ginny asked innocently.

I sighed. There was no sense in being rude.

"Guys, this is Nate," I said, gesturing behind me. "He lives in Birmingham and I met him in the casino last night. Nate, these are my friends."

"Hello," he said cheerfully.

To my dismay, Ginny jumped up from her lounge chair.

"I'm gonna go sit with Kiki," she said. "Give you guys a chance to chat."

Nate, who seemed amused by the entire situation, came and sat down on the lounger next to me.

"So," he said. "You're pretty annoyed by me, huh?"

"I am not!" I said, surprised.

"I'll leave you alone, if you want," he said, holding up his hands. "But I thought it would be cool to get to know you a little. No biggie, alright?"

"Okay," I said, feeling kind of childish for my behavior. "Look, I'm sorry if I'm coming across as rude. My friends are being a little annoying. They think I need to be set up."

"And you disagree?" Nate asked.

"Of course I disagree," I snapped. "I have absolutely no problem getting a guy myself."

He appraised me for a minute. In spite of myself, I felt a blush rise to my cheeks.

"You know what, Annie? I have no problem believing that at all."

I blushed harder and looked down. What the hell was my problem? I was so not the type of girl that got all red-faced over a guy. It was ridiculous.

"So is it okay with you if I hang out over here for a little while?" he asked. "My friends are right over there, and I'll go back and join them whenever you want, I promise. No pressure."

"Of course you can stay," I muttered. "I'm pretty boring, though. I have no plans to do anything but lay here in the sun for the foreseeable future."

"Sounds good to me," he said, settling back in the chair. "God, just think: in a few short months it's going to be snowing in Detroit."

I groaned. "Oh, hell, don't even say that."

"So, you live in Ferndale?" he asked, squinting over at me.

"Yup," I said. "I rent a house there with my friend Jen." I pointed her out. "And Ginny lives a few streets away. Kiki and Eric over there are married and they live in Birmingham too."

"Have you always lived around there?" he asked.

"Yeah. We grew up there," I explained. "What about you? You said you're from Birmingham, right?"

"Yeah, and don't think I didn't see you roll your eyes last night," he said, laughing. "What, you assume I'm a snob or something because I live in a nice town?"

I shifted, uncomfortable. To tell the truth, that was pretty much exactly what I thought. "Sorry," I told him. "I just went to college with a couple of people who live out that way. They were kind of stuck-up. I guess I'm a little prejudiced."

"No problem," he said. "I'm actually pretty new to Birmingham. I moved there from Maryland, for work."

"What do you do?" I asked.

"I'm an engineer," he said. "For Ford."

"Wow," I said. "That's pretty impressive."

"It's pretty nerdy," he laughed. I was surprised to find that I liked the sound. Usually the guys I went for weren't so quick to laugh. "I've always been into computers and math. It's fun for me to see the stuff I do on the computer actually get created, you know?"

"I can see that," I said. Hmm, he had surprised me again.

"So what do you do?" he asked.

"I'm an actress," I told him.

"I knew it!" he said, sitting up straight and pointing at me.

"The hell?" I asked, confused

"I knew I had seen you somewhere. You were in *Proof* last year, weren't you? At the Y?"

"Uh, yeah, I was," I said.

"I saw you!" he exclaimed, still pointing at me. "I saw that show! You were really, really good!"

I stared at him in shock. *Proof* was an awesome show, and it was the biggest role I'd had since college, but it had been a tiny little production at the YMCA. If I recalled correctly, I had been paid in vouchers from the restaurant down the street. "You saw that?" I asked Nate. And more to the point, he *remembered* me?

"Yeah! It was good. I enjoyed it." The expression on my face must have registered. "What?"

"Nothing," I said, shaking my head. "I'm just surprised. You don't strike me as the theater-going type."

"See, you shouldn't judge me until you get to know me," he said, pointing at me again.

Over his head, I caught Ginny staring at us, a huge grin on her face.

"So do you regularly go to local theater?" I asked, still feeling off-balance.

"Sometimes," he said. "I have a friend who loves that kind of stuff. I go with him once in a while. I like it. We've seen some great stuff."

"Wow," I said. "That's pretty cool."

"So what else have you done?" he asked, lying on his side so he was completely facing me now.

"Uh, nothing too big, to be honest. Not since college. I've had a few small roles here and there and I've done a bunch of backstage stuff, but nothing too exciting. It's been tough breaking into the scene, ya know?"

"I bet." He nodded. "But you were seriously really good. I mean, I still remembered you after a whole year. That's got to count for something. I bet it's only a matter of time."

I smiled at him. "Thanks. Actually," I paused, unsure if I should tell him. But he *had* seemed so genuinely interested in my acting. "Actually, I had a really big audition last week. Do you know Jenner Collins?"

"Pretty boy in the action movies?" he asked.

I wrinkled my nose at him. "I wouldn't quite describe him that way. He's from the area, did you know that? And he puts on a lot of really good shows with local talent."

"Well, I still think he's a pretty boy. But that's cool. So what's the deal with audition?"

"It was for one of Jenner's shows," I explained. "It goes up in a month and a half. And I got a callback."

"That's amazing!" Nate said. "Good for you. When's the callback?"

"It was last week," I admitted. "I think it went really well, but you never know."

"When will you find out?" he asked.

"It could be any day. The timing of this trip was really good for me, actually. Otherwise I'd be sitting at home obsessing."

"Yeah, it's good to have distractions when you're waiting for that kind of thing."

I looked over at his tanned, muscular body and smiled. "Yeah. Distractions can be really good."

Chapter Nine

"Annie, seriously, I need to get in there!" Ginny shouted from outside the bathroom door.

"One second!" I shouted back. "Stupid, fucking humidity..."

I attacked my hair with the straightener one last time before I gave up. It was a losing battle.

I exited the bathroom and found Ginny waiting for me. "If you say one word about my hair, I'll kill you, McKensie," I told her.

She rolled her eyes. "Your hair is fine," she said. "You always get so worked up over it. Most girls would kill to have curls like that."

"Frizz," I corrected. "I have frizz. Red frizz. And the heat around here isn't helping at all."

"Well, why are you bothering straightening it then?" she asked. "Why don't you just braid it? It will get it up off your face and it looks so pretty like that."

"We're in Vegas," I whined. "I want to look sexy and chic, not like a freaking librarian."

"Sexy and chic, huh?" she said, her face lighting up. "Who might we want to impress tonight, huh?"

"Oh, shut up," I said, scowling.

"Seriously, are you going to see him?" she asked.

I shrugged. "Who knows? I have plans with you guys."

Kiki's dad had included tickets to Cirque de Soleil in our package. I was really excited; it was supposed to be incredible.

"Yeah, but we're in Vegas," Ginny said impatiently. "It's not like you're gonna go up to bed as soon as the show is over."

"We might meet up at the fountain," I admitted. "But only if I feel like it. It wasn't set in stone or anything."

Ginny smirked. "Well, I hope that works out then," she said before she headed into the bathroom to do her own hair.

I decided to take Ginny's advice and just braid my hair. There was no point in fighting it. I sat down at the desk in front of a mirror and went to work on my hair. As I looked at myself in the mirror, I smiled a little goofily. It had been a great day so far. The truth was, I was really excited about the prospect of seeing Nate again. I'd had more fun with him by the pool then I cared to admit. When we had to leave to go the stratosphere tower, I actually felt disappointed. When he offered to meet up at the Bellagio fountains later that night, I was quick to agree.

And while the thrill rides at the top of the tower were crazy fun and terrifying, I'd had had a hard time keeping my mind off my date all day.

Get a hold of yourself, I instructed myself firmly. *He's not your boyfriend. It's a little fun to have on vacation, nothing more. Enjoy it, then move on.*

That had been my motto with boys for years, and it had always served me well. Unlike Ginny and Jen, I had spent little of our teens years pining for boys who didn't like me back. In our twenties, I'd had few moments of heartbreak. I just worked better that way.

A few minutes later, Ginny was ready. "See, babe," she said, looking me over. "You look great. Totally hot. Nate will love it...if, you know, you happen to see him."

I knew she was teasing me, but I ignored it. "Ready?" I asked her.

"Yup," she replied. "Let's go find the others."

***

Three hours later I was heading across the busy street toward the Bellagio casino. Even from this distance I could see people gathering for the dancing fountain's next performance. Ginny and I had seen the show from our room a few times, and I had to admit it was pretty cool. I wondered for a moment if Nate would be there. What if he was having too much fun with his friends? What if they had decided to get strippers after all?

Stop obsessing, I told myself. *It isn't you.*

As I hurried across the courtyard toward the fountain, I heard a voice.

"Annie!"

I turned, and there he was, walking toward me. He was dressed in a suit, but had removed his tie and unbuttoned the top few buttons of his shirt. I couldn't help the smile that broke out across my face. He looked great.

Before I could even say hello, he had reached for me and pulled me into a big hug. "I was getting worried you might ditch me," he said into my hair.

"Nah," I replied, smiling into his suit jacket. "I'm here."

He looked down at me, the lights from the strip reflecting off his hair. "I'm really, really glad," he said, his deep voice sending a flutter into my belly. He stared down at me for a minute and I again felt color spread to my cheeks. "Come on," he said finally. "I think the show is going to start soon."

We approached the crowd gathered around the fountain as the lights around the lake began to dim. The people fell silent and the music started.

"Hey, I know this music," I said as the operatic piece began. "It's *Time to Say Goodbye*—that's Sarah Brightman!"

Nate looked down at me with a bemused expression. "She was in *Phantom of the Opera*," I said sheepishly. "Sorry, theater dork."

He just grinned and put his arm around me.

From our room high above, Ginny and I could tell that the fountains would be cool. But I had no idea how amazing it would be in person like this, once the music got going. The jets were synchronized perfectly with the music, like the water was really dancing.

As the music reached its crescendo and the water pushed ever higher into the sky, I was surprised to find wetness on my cheeks. I looked up and saw that Nate was watching me rather than the show. "Sorry," I whispered, embarrassed. "It's beautiful."

"Don't be sorry," he said, shaking his head. "You're beautiful too."

I felt my stomach lurch in a disturbing way, so I just smiled at him. Now that the show had ended, the crowds around us began to disperse, and the spell seemed to be broken. "Alright," Nate said, as we started to move away from the fountain. "What do you feel like doing tonight? Did you already eat?"

I shook my head. "No, we had a huge lunch but our tickets for Cirque were right around dinner time."

"Then we should eat," he said, taking my hand. "What do you feel like?"

"I'd be up for anything," I said, shrugging.

"Well, that's good," he replied. "Because Vegas happens to be very well-known as one of the culinary capitals of the United States."

"Really?" I asked skeptically. "Isn't Vegas all about buffets and cheap casino comps?"

He gasped in mock horror. "Absolutely not! All of the great chefs have restaurants here. Bobby Flay, Wolfgang Puck, Joel Robuchon."

I raised my eyebrows at him. "Bobby Flay as in that guy from TV?"

Nate shook his head at me sadly. "Your culinary education is woefully lacking. You must allow me to rectify that for you."

"Oh my God, you're one of those foodie people, aren't you?" I asked. "Please don't tell me you're gonna take me to some place where the food is so fancy you don't even want to touch it and the portion is so small it would work better for Barbie doll. I'm a real girl, okay? I have an appetite. "

"Please," he said, tugging on my hand. "Just trust me. You're about to have the best meal of your life."

Chapter Ten

*'The first date is such an important part of your mate-finding experience. It is essential that you present yourself as the girl your new guy just can't live without. It's a good idea to eat something small before you leave; you wouldn't want to end up starving and stuffing your face in front of Mr. Right. What a turn-off! It's also a good idea to abstain from drinking. Only one glass of wine with dinner, if you must. A man looking for a wife isn't going to be interested in a beer-guzzler, ladies!'—**The Single Girl's Guide to Finding True Love**

"I was right, wasn't I?" Nate asked, watching my face closely as I chewed. I wanted to keep him in suspense for a while longer, but I couldn't help the little moan that escaped my lips.

"See!" he said triumphantly. "It's delicious, isn't it? I told you!"

I finished chewing and smiled at him. "Yeah, it was pretty damn good."

I was surprised when Nate had hailed a cab and taken us to this little restaurant set back from the craziness of the strip. It seemed a little bit like a dive to me, definitely not as fancy or chic as the places I had been frequenting thus far on my trip. But when Nate insisted we both order starters before I formed an opinion, I agreed. He had begged me to let him order for me, and his enthusiasm about my eating experience charmed me. I had ended up with some steak-wrapped artichoke thing. And to tell you the truth, it was one of the most delicious things I had ever eaten.

"So you want to stay and order?" he asked.

"If the entrees are as good as that starter, then I definitely want to stay."

He handed me the menu and I looked it over.

"What do you think?" he asked, his face lit up like a little kid at a toy store. I had to admit, it was kind of cute.

"It looks kind of eclectic," I said. I was no food expert (that was Jen's department) but even I could recognize a wide gamut of influences on this menu, from Italian to American to French.

"That's the beauty of it!" Nate said. "They're not bound by labels or traditions. They just make really good food."

"Okay, you're gonna need to chill out a little bit," I told him, laughing. "This place has already won me over. No need to oversell."

He laughed too. "Sorry, this is just one of my favorite restaurants."

"I didn't know you've been to Vegas before," I said, surprised he hadn't mentioned it.

"It was one of my dad's favorite vacations," he said quietly. I had a bad feeling about his expression.

"Is he...um, is he still around?" I asked tentatively.

"Naw," Nate said, taking a gulp of his water. "He died a few years ago. Heart attack."

"Nate, I'm really sorry to hear that," I said. I felt terrible. I should have just let the moment go.

"I am, too," he said, taking a deep breath. "He loved coming out here. He had me and my sisters here from the time we were kids. He would hit up the casinos while we hung out at the hotel. And then at night he would take us around to all of his favorite restaurants. I loved those vacations."

He seemed happy enough remembering it, and I breathed a sigh of relief. When he looked sad like that I had an overwhelming urge to wrap him up in a big hug. A thought that was way too maternal—not a very Annie-like inclination.

"What about you?" he asked, looking up at me. "Are both of your parents still around?"

Crap. I so did not want to talk about this. There was a reason I liked to keep things light with the guys I dated. But he had told me about his dad and it would be pretty rude not to reciprocate.

"Um, my parents split up when I was younger," I explained, trying to get it over with quickly. "My mom brought me up. She's still around; she lives pretty close to Jen and me. But I don't see my dad."

"Really?" he asked, sounding surprised. "Like, not at all?"

I shook my head, wishing he would drop it. I hated talking about my dad. "Nope, haven't seen him in years."

"I'm sorry, Annie," he said, and I hated the pity in his voice. I had to remind myself that what he had been through was worse.

"It's not a big deal. Like I said, it happened when I was little," I replied. Where the hell was our waiter? If this line of conversation continued, I was going to be desperate for a beer in no time.

"How's your mom?" he asked. "You guys pretty close?"

I sighed, starting to feel irritated. Why did people always feel the need to have these drawn-out question-and-answer sessions?

"We're not very close," I replied flatly, hoping he would catch my tone. "We don't have a lot in common and she can't believe that I could be happy without being married."

"My mom is like that, too," Nate said, laughing. His lightness surprised me. "She's determined to marry me and my sisters off. Probably because she feels bad for us, being fatherless and all. Its like she's desperate for us to have families of our own."

I smiled in spite of myself. "That sounds just like my mom," I said. "It's annoying, but what can you do?"

The waiter finally returned to take our dinner orders. I decided on the lobster ravioli while Nate asked for a steak. I also made sure to order a large beer.

"So," Nate said. "You clearly want to change the subject."

I had to laugh. He had a knack for reading my mood, that was for sure. "Why don't you tell me about your friends? You guys seem pretty close."

My mood brightened considerably after that. I could talk about Ginny and Jen all day. By the time the server returned with our food, we were laughing and I was having fun again.

"How do you feel about cheesecake?" Nate asked once my plate was cleared. Like the very ladylike girl that I was, I had eaten every single bite of my delicious lobster ravioli.

"I adore cheesecake," I said. "My friend Jen actually makes the best cheesecake in the world."

Nate shook his head seriously. "I've never had Jen's cheesecake, but I think I need to challenge it. The chef here is the cheesecake master. It's so good you might cry."

"Okay," I said, grinning at him. "Bring it on."

***

After dinner, Nate suggested we find a bar to relax in. "Unless you're in the mood for dancing?" he asked solicitously.

"Naw," I replied. "I'm too stuffed for dancing."

Nate had been right about the cheesecake, but I made him promise not to tell Jen that I thought so.

We ended up at the Extra Lounge, one of several clubs in our hotel. It was packed, which was hardly surprising for a Saturday night. We found ourselves at a high-top crammed back in a corner. I couldn't complain about the accommodations—the close quarters meant that I was practically on top of Nate.

The strange thing about Nate is that the more I got to know him, the more I liked him. Usually my experience was the polar opposite. But I was starting to think that his kindness and his interest were actually genuine.

Just listen to yourself, I thought. *Carrying on like this might turn serious. It's just some fun.*

Nate kept the drinks coming all night. I knew I should probably slow down, but I was having such a good time with him. Between the buzz of people in the bar, the alcohol, and the intensity in his eyes when he looked at me—well, it was all getting very heady.

"Tell me about your favorite trip ever," Nate said, leaning over the table. I screwed up my face.

"I gotta say, this one will be hard to beat," I told him. "I haven't really traveled much. Never had the money growing up...or since, for that matter."

He chuckled. "That's rough," he said. "I love to travel."

"I wish I could more often. Before this, the most exciting trip I'd taken was with Ginny, Jen, and Danny over to Lake Michigan. It was a disaster. It rained the entire time and they messed up our reservations. And Danny was a little terror."

"That sucks," he laughed. "Well, all the more reason to make this an amazing vacation."

When he said it, he caught my eye, staring at me intently. I felt my stomach lurch. If I leaned forward, just a little bit, I'd be kissing him.

Just as I was about to act on the impulse, my phone beeped, surprising me so much I nearly fell off the chair.

"Whoa," Nate said, grabbing my arm to keep me upright.

"Thanks," I said, looking down at the screen. "Text from Ginny."

"Checking up on you?" he asked.

"Making sure I'm okay," I corrected. "We have a long-standing rule about checking in when we're out with strange men."

"I'm a strange man now?" he asked. "I think I'm offended."

"All men are strange," I replied, winking at him.

He moved a little closer and bumped my shoulder with his. Mmm. Very muscular shoulder. It felt great against mine. I had a flash of the way he had looked in his swimsuit down by the pool and felt an urge to get closer to him.

To distract myself, I opened the message and read it.

"She's wondering when I'll be back," I told him. He didn't respond. When I looked up, his eyes were trained on my lips. The look on his face sent a rush straight through my chest.

"Why don't you tell her you *won't* be in tonight," he said, his voice low.

I felt my heart start to beat faster as I met his eyes. He was so gorgeous in that moment that it almost took my breath away.

"Okay," I whispered, feeling totally blown away by him. "I'll tell her."

Chapter Eleven

*'Ladies, we should talk about the sensitive issue of relations. When a man compliments you, it might be tempting to offer yourself to him in an intimate way. I cannot warn against this strenuously enough! It is so important that you remain a mystery to the man you wish to end up with. There's an old saying about cows and milk—truer words were never spoken, ladies! Just remember that when you're feeling insecure.'—**The Single Girl's Guide to Finding True Love**†*

I woke up in the morning even more hung over than I had been the day before. "Ginny," I moaned into the pillow. "What the hell did I drink?"

"Ginny isn't here," an amused male voice said next to me. I sat up straight in bed, ready to scream my head off. Who in the...

"Oh my God, Nate" I gasped. "You scared the *hell* out of me."

"Forget where you were?" he asked. "I think I'm a little offended."

"Sorry," I said, placing my hand over my heart in an effort to calm it. "I was just confused."

"You did have quite a bit to drink," he said. "I hope I didn't take advantage of you." He was doing that amused looking smile thing that was becoming so familiar to me, and I felt myself smile in return.

"I don't think that's possible."

"Yeah," he agreed. "In fact, I think it was probably the other way around. I'm feeling a little violated here, Annie."

I giggled, and leaned over to kiss him. "Sorry 'bout that. Can I make it up to you?"

"What did you have in mind?" he asked, a glint in his eye.

"Hmm," I said, thinking of the options. "I could help you out in the shower, scrub your back for you..."

He gasped. "Miss Duncan, my virgin ears!"

I laughed and stood up, letting the blanket fall away from my body, knowing full well that I had lost my dress in a heap by the door last night. "If you'd rather stay in bed, that's fine. But you know where to find me."

I left him laughing in the bed as I headed to the bathroom. I had almost reached the door when I heard the springs move and his feet hit the floor. I smiled, and waited for him to catch up to me.

**

"And where were you last night?" Matt asked, raising his eyebrow at me as I entered my suite an hour later. He and Jen were lounging on my bed while Ginny was searching through her suitcase. She stood up to look at me as I entered the room.

"Hussy," she said, grinning. "So, how was it?"

"Oh, shut up," I said, but couldn't keep the grin off my face.

"I knew it!" Jen shouted. "You're totally into him, aren't you?"

"He's very nice," I said, playing shy.

Matt laughed. "Coy doesn't suit you, sweetie." I flipped him off. "Now *there's* the Annie we all know and love," he said.

"So when do we get to hang out with him?" Jen asked.

"Well he was gonna maybe tag along with us today, if that's cool with you guys," I said, going over to the closet to find a sundress.

"Of course it is," Ginny said.

"What about his friends?" Matt asked. "Isn't he here for some bachelor party or something?"

I shrugged. "He didn't say that it would be a problem."

"Well, good," Ginny said. "Because he obviously likes you a lot."

I looked away quickly.

"Oh my God," Matt cried, pointing at me. "She's blushing! Annie Duncan is actually blushing. I've never seen that before!"

"You guys all suck," I muttered, grabbing my sundress and heading to the bathroom amongst gales of their laughter.

***

We met up with Kiki and Eric down at the breakfast buffet. I was ravenous and loaded up on waffles and sausage before I joined the group at our table.

"Annie!" Kiki squealed when she saw me. "Oh my God, Jen just told me all about it!"

I saw Matt, who was sitting closest to her, rub his ear. I couldn't blame him—she was in high-pitched Kiki mode.

"Calm down," I told her, looking around at all the people now staring at us. "It's not a big deal."

"But Jen said he's totally into you and you were blushing this morning talking about it. I know you, Annie Duncan. You are not the blushing type. That means it must be a huge deal!"

"Aw," a voice in my ear said, and I spun around. Nate was right next to me, leaning down so his face was at my level. "You were blushing? About me? How cute."

I could have died. I glared at Kiki, who had the good grace to look mortified. "Sorry," she mouthed. I noticed that the others were trying hard not to laugh.

"Hey," I said shortly, turning my face away from him. "Did you eat?"

"I've got my plate right here," he said, turning to the empty table behind us and grabbing a full plate. "Mind if I join you?"

"Oh, go right ahead," I said drily. A waiter passed our table with a full tray of mimosas, and I flagged him down, grabbing two.

"Are you sure you're feeling okay, Annie?" Ginny asked. "You seem a little on edge."

I'm going to kill you, I thought, staring straight at her.

I knew what my friends were doing. I guess I had a bit of a reputation as a smart-ass. I know I had a tendency to tease people and make light of things—but that was part of my charm! Now they seemed determined to have their revenge. And they were clearly having a great time with it, from the looks of things.

"So, what's on the agenda for today?" I asked, with what I felt was supreme dignity.

"Ooh, I have lots of ideas!" Kiki said. "I want to go shopping here at the hotel. They have this mall, the Miracle Mile, that's supposed to be amazing. And then

I want to see the botanical gardens at the Bellagio. And we never did eat at Bobby Flay's. Oh, and then we have to try to catch the views from the top of the Eiffel Tower. God, I can't believe we're leaving in the morning! This trip went way too fast."

Under the table, Nate caught my hand and squeezed it. I felt my anxiety dissipate immediately, as if I was reassured somehow, more comfortable.

"I'm going to need more pool time," Ginny said, peering toward the windows. "It will start getting cold so soon at home."

"I know," Jen moaned. "How did it get to be September already?"

"Okay, so shopping, botanical gardens, and pool time," Eric said, looking down at his watch. "We better get a move on it then. That's a lot of stuff to fit into one afternoon."

The shopping at our casino *was* pretty awesome. I have no idea how they managed to fit an entire mall in there with everything else that was in the building. At the Michael Kors store, I stared around at the accessories in awe. There was a silver bag that I couldn't keep my eyes off. I wanted that purse more than I'd ever wanted a purse in my life.

But when Nate offered to buy it for me, I was horrified. I did not let guys do things like that.

"No," I told him firmly. "I mean, thanks, but no."

"It's a gift, Annie," he said, shaking his head with that amused glint in his eyes. "It's not a huge deal."

"It is," I told him. "I've only known you for a few days, and that bag is really expensive."

He merely shrugged his shoulders. "Whatever you want," he said.

After a few hours, even Ginny had had enough of shopping. Kiki was eager to check out the botanical gardens, but the rest of us were feeling pretty rough and decided to go straight to the pool. I realized that I wasn't the only one nursing a hangover.

"Oh, man," Ginny said, as a waiter brought her a giant pink and white concoction with an umbrella. "This looks incredible." She took a deep gulp and moaned. "So good."

"What is it?" I asked, looking at the drink with interest.

"A Miami Vice," the server replied. "Half pina-colada, half strawberry daiquiri."

"Yeah, we'll need a couple more of those," Jen said. The waiter smiled and went off to get our drinks.

A few moments later, stretched out on the lounger with a Miami Vice in my hand, my headache was totally forgotten. "This is heaven," I said to no one in particular. "Seriously, if you lived here how would you ever get anything done?"

"It's pretty hot though," Jen said, wiping at her forehead. "I mean, we're just laying around and I'm already sweating. My hair is getting messed up."

Under my sunglasses, I rolled my eyes. Classic Jen.

A few minutes later, I was regretting my internal mocking of her. It *was* really hot. "Ugh, I'm all sticky," I said after I had drained the last of my drink. "I think I need to hop in the pool."

"I'll go with you," Nate said lazily.

I walked over to the edge and contemplated the water. It probably wasn't too cold, not with the sun beating down like this.

Before I could out-think myself, I jumped right in. I swam under the water for a few minutes, luxuriating in the feel of the cool liquid against my heated skin.

When I resurfaced, Nate was standing right next to me in the water, grinning.

"You're not like other girls, Annie Duncan. Has anyone ever told you that?"

"Multiple times," I said drily.

"Do you know how many girls I know that would refuse to jump in a pool because they're too scared of getting their hair wet?" he asked.

I rolled my eyes. "I'm not a girly girl," I told him, feeling slightly defensive, though I couldn't tell why. "Sorry if that disappoints you."

He grabbed me around the waist, pulling me close to him. "I love it," he said softly, before kissing me.

I knew that my friends were probably sitting there watching me, probably coming up with more ammunition to tease me with. I tried to pull back, but the insistency of Nate's lips kept me locked in place. Finally, I decided to just give in to it. After all, he was a really good kisser.

And my friends could just eat their hearts out.

Chapter Twelve

The last full day in Vegas passed in a blur. After we'd had enough of the pool we went inside to change for the afternoon. We did one more round at the buffet ("I'll miss this so much when I have to start cooking again," Ginny sighed) then headed off to the Eiffel Tower to check out the views of the strip. In the evening we had reservations at Bobby Flay's restaurant, as well as tickets for some comedy show.

In the evening, Nate had to go and eat with his friends. He said he was neglecting them. When I apologized for occupying so much of his time, he waved me off.

"They don't really care," he said. "They've all been drunk pretty much twenty-four-seven. Besides, they know how unlikely it is for me to fall for someone like this."

His words sent a jolt of panic through me. He wasn't serious, was he? I mean, we had only known each other for a few days. He couldn't actually think he was falling for me.

"Anyhow," he said. "I think we're planning to go see the comedy show as well. Wanna meet up there? And then maybe we could hang out after?"

I wondered if I should refuse him. It freaked me out, what he had said. Would it be better to put the kibosh on this whole thing right now?

"Annie," he said softly, kissing my neck just below my ear. It made me shiver. What had I been feeling so worried about? It was hard to remember.

"Did you hear me?" he whispered. "I asked if you wanted to meet up later."

"Mmmhmm," I murmured, not really caring too much about my objections anymore. "That sounds great."

**

The whole group did some casino-hopping after the comedy club. Nate stayed close by me throughout the night. He even taught me how to play a few of the games. With him teaching me, I had to admit it was a lot more fun than I had thought it was the first night. I even won a bit of money at blackjack.

"This is awesome!" I told him as I turned my hundred-dollar chip over in my hand. "I don't think I've ever won anything before!"

He kissed me.

"What was that for?" I asked him

"Nothing," he replied. "You can just be really, really cute when you let your guard down a little."

I had no idea how to take that, so I just rolled my eyes. "Whatever," I told him. "Let's go try our luck on the slot machines."

I spent the night with Nate again, lying awake for a long time after he had fallen asleep. It felt really nice in his arms, really comfortable. I knew that it was a feeling I could get used to.

There was a part of me that was starting to dread the next morning, when we would have to say goodbye. It was ridiculous—I barely knew him. And I wasn't interested in a relationship anyhow. But nonetheless, I got a little pain in my stomach when I thought about it. *It must just be that you don't want the vacation to end*, I told myself. It made me feel better.

Suddenly, it dawned on me that I hadn't thought about my callback all day. I had been having such a good time, and had been so caught up in Nate, that it had completely escaped my mind. For some reason, the realization scared me. What was I doing? There was nothing more important to me than my career, besides the girls and Danny. Why on earth was I allowing myself to forget that, even for a minute?

I suddenly felt claustrophobic in Nate's arms. I yearned for my own bed, in my own room. As quietly as I could, so I wouldn't disturb him, I started to wiggle out of his grasp. I had almost made it to the edge of the bed when he woke up.

"Hey," he said, smiling at me in the darkness. "Where ya going?"

"Nowhere," I whispered. "Just getting a drink."

"Well, hurry back," he said.

I found a glass on the desk and took it to the bathroom to fill it. I stared at myself in the mirror. My fair skin had taken on a lot of color down here in the hot sun. My hair was pulled back in a braid and little wisps were escaping around my face. It made my face look softer, not so familiar. In fact, I hardly recognized myself there in Nate's room.

I walked back to bed, hoping he had fallen asleep. No such luck.

"Get over here," he murmured, pulling me close and kissing me.

"I thought you were sleeping," I told him.

"I was. But now I'm awake. And so are you. And if we're both awake, why are we wasting the little time we have talking?"

I laughed. "How about we spend it sleeping in this crazy comfortable bed? I have an early flight tomorrow."

"Oh, you poor thing," he said, pushing me onto my back and kissing my neck. "She has to fly home on a luxurious private jet. Never mind that some of us will be slumming it in coach."

It was hard to concentrate when he was kissing me like that. Not for the first time, I had the sensation of my mind being wiped clean, all the worries and anxieties fading into the background. "You're a dangerous boy, Nate Hughes."

"Me?" he asked, laughing against my skin. "I'm one of the nice boys, Annie. I'd imagine we don't look all that familiar to you, but take my word for it." Then he was kissing me again, and I decided that talking was overrated.

Nate was right, of course. He was one of the nice ones.

But that sure didn't mean he wasn't dangerous.

***

When I woke up in the morning, I had that horrible Monday morning feeling. Like I used to feel when my mom would wake me up for school— particularly on those mornings after I had snuck out with Jen and Ginny the night before.

"I can't believe we have to go home," I moaned, burying my face in the pillow.

"It sucks," Nate agreed, wrapping his arm around me and snuggling into my side. "But it helps knowing you'll be there when I get back."

"I...what?" I asked, caught off guard.

"Your flight leaves first, right?" he asked. "So by the time I get home, you'll already be there. That makes it a little easier to head back."

I was stunned. We hadn't talked at all about what would happen when we left this city. Was he assuming we would pick up where we left off? Sure, I had totally lost my head with him the last few days. It seemed like all he had to do was kiss me and I would forget about all of my objections.

But in the cold light of morning, they were all coming back to me.

"Hey," Nate said, pulling my face away from the pillow. "Why aren't you talking? What's going on?"

"Nothing," I said, trying to quell the flash of fear I was feeling. "I just...I didn't realize you would still want to see me. At home, I mean."

"Why wouldn't I want to see you?" he asked, bewildered.

"I don't know. I guess I just thought..."

"What, Annie?" he asked, an edge to his voice.

"I just thought this was a bit of fun, you know? A vacation fling."

He was silent for a moment and I couldn't meet his eyes.

"It was fun," he finally agreed, his voice measured. "I think we're good together. So why can't that fun continue in Detroit?"

I finally looked up at him. His expression was a little worrying—almost like he was trying too hard to be casual.

"Nate...I don't really date. I'm just not into it. There's so much going on at home right now; work, and the audition. I don't...I don't think I would want anything to get serious."

87

Why was it so hard to tell him all of this? I'd had this conversation with a ton of guys over the years.

"That's fine, Annie," he said, staring at me with an intensity I couldn't place. "There's no pressure. We have fun, right? Let's just keep our options open."

I stared hard into his eyes, trying to decide if he was serious or not. Finally, his face broke out into a huge grin. "Oh, relax, woman. I'm not going to start stalking you or something. I just want to take you out once in a while."

It did seem pretty silly, when he put it like that. I grinned back and wrapped my arms around his neck. "I can deal with that," I said, leaning up to kiss him.

Chapter Thirteen

"Going home sucks," Ginny said, plopping her bag down on the floor of my living room. "Why the hell do we live in this cold-ass state anyhow?"

"Oh, you would hate it if you didn't get to experience the seasons," Jen said, walking past us to put her bag in her room.

"I would not," Ginny muttered.

"I do love fall," I admitted, sitting on the couch. "When the air gets all crisp and the leaves change color. We can take Danny to the apple orchard. He would love that."

"True," Ginny said, sitting down next to me. "But winter can suck it."

"Speaking of Danny," Jen said, rejoining us in the living room. "When are they coming to get you?"

"Ready to be done with me?" Ginny asked, raising an eyebrow.

"Yeah, right," Jen said. "I just have a present for the baby, I'm excited to see him."

"Ooh, what'd you get him?" Ginny asked, sitting up straighter. I could tell that the topic of her son had already cheered her up.

"A shirt, a few toys; nothing too major," Jen said.

"Hmm, that sounds like what I got him," I said.

Ginny looked at me, a slightly sheepish smile on her face. "Me, too. I think we went a little overboard."

Rachel Schurig

When Josh and Danny arrived a few minutes later, it was clear that we had gone more than just a little overboard. After accepting kisses and hugs from all three of us, Danny was promptly made to open no fewer than ten presents. He was now the proud owner of four Vegas t-shirts, an Eiffel Tower money bank, several pool floats in various shapes, and a gladiator costume from Caesar's Palace.

"Talk about spoiled," Josh muttered. "Is anyone at all excited to see *me*?"

Ginny ceased her incessant kissing of Danny to smile at Josh. "Sorry, babe," she said, getting up to hug him hello. Jen took over snuggling the baby. I had to admit, Josh had a point. Between the three women in his life, Danny was pretty spoiled. But how could you blame us, when he was that cute and sweet?

"Oh."

We all looked up to see Tina standing in the doorway, looking at us with a bewildered expression.

"There are people here," she said, still looking confused.

"Hey, Tina," Jen said. "How was your weekend?"

"Weekend?" she asked, her fake airy voice becoming more pronounced.

"Yeah, your weekend," Jen said. "Did you enjoy having the house to yourself while we were gone?"

"You were gone?" Tina asked.

I rolled my eyes. She was such a faker.

"Yeah, we've been in Vegas, remember? You said goodbye to us when we left on Thursday," I said.

"Oh...oh, yes, I suppose I do remember that. It must have slipped my mind. I've been doing so much meditating, I've barely been on this plane at all..."

With a dreamy little shrug, she turned and slipped back to her bedroom. Jen and Ginny were doing their damnedest not to laugh. "She is *ridiculous*," I muttered. "Seriously, who does she think she's kidding?"

"I'm surprised you don't like her," Josh said, draping his arm lazily over Ginny's shoulder. "I mean, aren't you supposed to be all into that open-minded hippie stuff? I've seen some of the theater friends you hang out with, you know."

"Tina is *not* a hippie," I said firmly. "She doesn't really believe in meditation or crystals or any of it. I would respect her if I thought she was for real, but she's not anything but a fake. Her whole persona is just an excuse to smoke pot and be lazy. She's a poser."

"The worst thing you can be in Annie's book," Ginny told him, smiling at me in a fond sort of way.

"Enough about crazy Tina," Josh said, leaning in for another kiss. "I thought you were supposed to be telling me how much you miss me?"

Ginny giggled and snuggled into him.

My cell phone rang, distracting me from the sight of Ginny and Josh reuniting. Something about the sight of them set off a little pain in my stomach, though I had no idea why—usually their overt displays of affection simply made me nauseous.

I looked down at the screen of my phone and found myself smiling involuntarily.

I managed to slip out of the living room without interrogation, and I answered the phone on my way to my bedroom.

"Hey," I said softly.

"Hey," Nate replied. I felt my smile grow. "Will you call me a wuss if I told you that I miss you already?"

"Probably," I said.

"Well, I guess I couldn't expect any less from you." The amusement was clear in his voice and I could just tell he was smiling on the other end of the phone. I felt my own smile grow wider. I probably looked like an idiot.

"What can I say, Nate? I'm a tough broad."

He laughed. "I'm actually not so sure about that."

"Really?"

"Yeah. I think that's just reputation, a cover."

"So what am I covering up?" I asked, feeling my stomach squirm a little at the flirtatious tone in his voice.

"Your soft and gooey underside," he replied. I burst out laughing.

"Nice try," I told him.

"I still think I'm right," he replied easily. "But I guess we can table the topic for now. So, are you home yet?"

"Yeah, landed about an hour ago. We're currently showering Danny with way too many gifts. You'd think it was his birthday or something."

"See?" Nate replied. "Even the baby has you wrapped around his finger. Soft and gooey, just like I said."

"Whatever," I said, rolling my eyes. "So where are you?"

"Waiting at the airport," he said. "Bored out of my mind and wishing you were here."

"What about all of your friends?" I asked.

"They're all hung over," he replied. "Everyone is sitting around with sunglasses on, trying not to move so they don't throw up."

"Sounds like a successful bachelor party," I said.

"I guess so. But anyhow, I wondered what you were up to tonight."

"Tonight?" I asked. I had been planning on lazing around the house, spending time with the girls and Danny.

"Yeah. I was thinking maybe we could get dinner when I get back."

When I didn't answer, he sighed. "Just casual, Annie," he said. "No big deal, I promise. We'll get dinner and I'll take you right home."

"Well, I do have to work tomorrow," I said, seizing on the excuse.

"Me too."

"But a person does have to eat..."

"Also true," Nate said, and I could once again hear the amusement in his voice. He knew I was caving.

"Fine," I said. "When does your flight land?"

"I can be in Ferndale by seven," he replied.

"Then I guess I'll see you at seven."

Nate was laughing outright now. "What?" I asked, feeling annoyed.

"Soft and gooey," he repeated.

"Goodbye, Nate," I muttered.

"Bye, Annie."

I could still hear the sounds of his quiet laughter as I ended the call.

***

I saw Nate three times over the next three days. I knew I was being stupid, allowing myself to move so fast with him, but I couldn't help it. If I was honest with myself, I really liked spending time with him. And it was, admittedly, very flattering to see how much he clearly liked spending time with me. He took me out to dinner the Sunday night we got back, again the following day, and met me for lunch on Tuesday.

That was another thing about Nate: he insisted on paying for everything. It made me feel uncomfortable. I had never been the type of girl to blindly let the guy take care of everything, and I told him so.

"What are you talking about?" he asked, sounding hurt. "I'm just trying to be a gentleman."

"But that implies that you think I need you to, like, provide for me or something."

Nate rolled his eyes. "Oh, please. I can tell that you are perfectly capable of taking care of yourself. But I'm the one who asked you out. And I was raised to believe that when you ask someone out, you pay. You can pay when you ask me out."

"Who said I'm ever going to ask you out?" I asked.

"No one said you had to," he replied, smirking. "But if you don't, I'll just keep asking you. Which means that I'll keep paying for your dinner. If you don't like it, I guess you'll have to do something about it."

I glared at him. "This all sounds like a ploy to make sure I'll keep seeing you."

He merely shrugged, the smirk still evident in his face.

At the end of our lunch date, he asked if I would see him for dinner. I was grateful for the excuse to decline—I knew I needed to slow this down, and fast. Luckily, I was babysitting for Danny that night so Ginny and Josh could have an evening to themselves.

"Okay," Nate said, nonplussed. "Tomorrow then?"

I looked at him with a raised eyebrow. "How about I take you out?" I asked.

Nate grinned broadly. "See?" he said. "My plan is totally working."

Chapter Fourteen

*'The first time your potential mate invites you to his home is a big deal. You can tell a lot about a man by the house he keeps. Does he care for his space? Is he good at making home repairs? Does it look like his home is dying for a woman's touch? Finding the answers to these questions can be very helpful in your quest to make your man fall for you.'—**The Single Girl's Guide to Finding True Love***

I took Nate to a low-key wine bar in Ferndale. The prices were reasonable but the food was really good. It had been a standby for me and the girls in our leaner financial times. Come to think of it, I was still experiencing those lean times. It seemed like everyone else was starting to settle down, make some real money. Why was I still broke?

I lamented this fact to Nate over dinner. "Being poor sucks," I said.

"Yeah, but if you're happy, does it really matter?" he asked. "Take me, for example. When I first moved out here and started working at Ford, I was making a ton of money."

I scowled at him. "You're making me feel so much better."

"Sorry." He grinned. "I just meant that I was making good money, but I was pretty damn miserable. I missed my family and my friends from home. It wasn't until I started hanging out with some guys from work and meeting new people that I could really enjoy myself. The money didn't really come into play."

"That's a good point," I mused, taking an onion ring from his plate. "I do have awesome friends. But my job sucks. It would be one thing to make crap money and have a job I love, you know? But to hate my job and be poor? That's just depressing."

"Then change it," he said simply. "If you don't like your job, find a new one."

"There aren't a lot of theater jobs," I said, reaching for my shiraz. "I feel like I have to stick to where I am or leave the business entirely."

"No way," Nate said, shaking his head. "You're way too talented. I bet you get that part in Jenner Collins' show. Then everything will be different."

I smiled at him, feeling unexpectedly touched. He seemed so sure of his words, so confident in my ability. I felt my stomach clench. I still hadn't heard back from the theater about my callback. A friend of mine from college was dating a lighting designer who had heard a rumor that Jenner Collins was holding a final round of auditions that night. The rumor, even coming third-hand, made me incredibly nervous. If they were holding more auditions that must mean that they didn't find what they were looking for at my callback.

"Hey," Nate said softly, grabbing my hand. I looked up at him. "It's going to be okay, Annie." It was like he had read my mind. The sincerity in his face made my breath catch.

"Let's get out of here," he continued. "We can go back to my place for another drink."

For once, I didn't argue with him. I was dying to see his apartment. Plus, the idea of being alone when I was feeling so unsure about things was not appealing.

Something about Nate's company made me feel calmer, less anxious. I had no desire to leave it so soon.

Nate drove the short distance to Birmingham in his Ford Focus. As I settled into the passenger seat, I realized for the first time that his car was less flashy than I would have expected. When I mentioned this, he laughed.

"I work for Ford, Annie. What did you expect me to drive, a jag?"

We pulled up in front of a modest, clean-looking apartment building. Also not quite what I had expected. When he had told me he lived in Birmingham I had pictured one of the rambling old houses that line the streets around the downtown area, or one of the ridiculously expensive lofts that marketed itself as being 'urban'. This building looked like it could happily exist in any small city in the area.

He led me up the stairs to a second floor apartment, unlocking the door and allowing me to enter first into the foyer. It opened directly into a spacious living room. Nate had furnished it better than most guys I knew: he actually had things like end tables and framed art on the walls. There was even a nice potted spider plant on the counter. Not a cheesy movie poster in sight.

"So this is how an engineer lives, huh?" I asked, looking around the room.

"Yup," Nate said, throwing his keys down on the side table. "There's a special store we shop at and everything."

"Hmm," I said, walking around the room to get a better look. "It's much cleaner than I expected."

He laughed. "Do I strike you as a messy person?"

"Most guys are," I said, picking up a picture frame and peering down at it. "Who's this?"

"Wow, you *are* nosey, aren't you?"

"I'm just trying to get a feel for it," I told him. "How does a young bachelor live on the other side of the poverty line."

He burst out laughing. "You really do think I'm a snob, don't you?"

"Nate, you wear a tie to work everyday," I pointed out. "I mean, come on."

He came over to me, wrapping his arms around me and pulling me tight. "You like my ties," he said, resting his forehead against mine. "Admit it."

"Never," I murmured, raising my face for a kiss.

"Nuh-uh," he said. "No kisses until you admit it. You like me in a suit."

"Fine," I conceded as he pulled me even closer. "I like you in a suit."

"Thought so," he murmured, his mouth inches from mine. Then he was kissing me, and any objection I may have had toward his ties was long gone.

We were interrupted by the sound of Nate's cell phone. He groaned against my mouth before releasing me. "I should get that," he said. "I'm expecting to hear from one of my coworkers."

As he rummaged through his jacket pockets for his phone, I continued my exploration of his apartment. It was very clean, and surprisingly put-together. His walls were not the institutional beige of most apartments of this caliber; instead they were painted in soft blues and grays. I wondered if he had painted them himself, and allowed myself a smile at the mental image of Nate at the home goods store planning his color scheme.

I wandered into the bedroom. Nate had a large queen-sized bed, neatly made up with a blue and green plaid comforter—another surprise. While I occasionally made my bed while cleaning my room, I rarely did so on a regular basis. I pictured him getting ready for work, rushing around in an unbuttoned dress shirt, making some coffee and grabbing some toast to eat. Then taking the time to make his bed before he left. The thought made me smile.

Then again, maybe he had only made the bed because he knew I would be here tonight.

I walked back to the living room. Nate was sitting at his dining table, deep in conversation on his cell phone. He waved to me as I entered and rolled his eyes a little in apology.

I walked over to his bookshelf, examining the titles. You can tell a lot about a person by the books they keep on their shelf. His was eclectic, a mix of classics and modern thrillers.

My attention was caught by a leather-bound photo album on the bottom shelf. I picked it up and went over to the couch. Opening to the front of the book, I found photo after photo of   Nate smiling up at me. He looked younger in most of them, and I suspected they were from his high school and college years. Pictures of Nate with an older couple (his parents?) in front of a Christmas tree, Nate dressed in a ski suit on a white-covered slope, Nate standing with a group of guys in shorts around a bonfire. A typical, middle-class life of a fairly happy and popular guy.

As I flicked through the pages, I began to notice a trend. There were a lot of pictures here of Nate with women. A few looked like they could be friends, or even his sisters. But there were several shots of reoccurring females, arms wrapped possessively around his waist.

Hard for you to fall for someone, eh? I thought to myself. It sure didn't look that way. From this photo album alone I could pick out at least five females who had almost definitely been Nate's girlfriends. All within the last few years.

It wasn't that I was jealous. It really didn't matter to me who he had seen, particularly not before I had even known him. But it did serve as a reminder—he'd been around this block before. However he might act like I was special or different, whatever he might say about a lack of girlfriends—all of that was possibly, probably even, an act. A line. Designed to make me feel special and get past my guard.

As I carefully returned the album to its shelf, my own phone rang. Not wanting to disturb Nate's work call, I headed back towards his room before I answered.

"Hello?"

"Hello, Miss Duncan? This is Jenner Collins."

It felt like my heart stopped for a second before it began pounding much more rapidly then it had been. "Hello, Mr. Collins," I said, struggling to keep my voice steady.

"Please, call me Jenner," he said easily.

"Only if you call me Annie," I said, in the most pleasant voice I could muster, all the while screaming on the inside for him to get on with it.

"Well, Annie," he said, "I'm calling to offer you the role of Jillian in my production of *The Curtain and the Window*."

My fingers immediately went numb and I was sure I was about to drop the phone. Was this real? Surely I was dreaming. Jenner Collins—Jenner Collins!—could not possibly be on the other end of my phone offering me a role in his play. It just wasn't possible.

"Annie?" he asked. "You still there?"

"I...I...yes, I'm here," I stammered, my throat dry. "Sorry...I..." *Pull yourself together!* I ordered. *Don't you dare blow this.*

"Sorry, Jenner," I said, my voice stronger now. "This comes as a pretty big shock to me. I would be thrilled to play Jillian."

"Wonderful!" he said, sounding amused. I wondered if he had some inkling of the total freak-out occurring in my head. "I'm glad to hear it. Now, we're on a very short rehearsal schedule, unfortunately. Some opportunities have come up that are going to push the production dates forward a bit. I'll explain it all at rehearsal, but we'd like to start tomorrow. Five o'clock. Can you clear your schedule?"

"Absolutely," I told him, nodding my head rapidly before I realized he couldn't see me. "That won't be a problem at all."

"Great," he replied. "We'll be switching up rehearsal spaces for a few weeks until we can get into the theater on a regular basis. My assistant is going to send you an email with the details."

"That sounds good," I said, gripping the phone tighter. It still felt like it was about to slip out of my fingers.

"Then I'll see you tomorrow, Annie."

"I'm looking forward to it," I replied. "Thank you so much."

We said goodbye and I ended the call. I stared down at my phone in shock, still hardly daring to believe the call had actually happened.

I don't know how long I stood like that, staring at my phone, before I finally heard the sound of Nate's voice.

"Annie?" he asked, standing in the doorway to his bedroom. "What's up?"

I realized then that I was shaking. Literally shaking. I couldn't believe that this was happening to me. It was the moment I had dreamt of my entire life.

"Annie?" he asked again, more sharply. "What's wrong?"

I looked up at Nate and felt the urge to tell him, to scream it at him, to throw my arms around him and ask him to celebrate with me.

Then it hit me. What the hell was I doing? My life was about to change and I was in some strange guy's bedroom? I should be sharing this with Jen and Ginny, no one else. Not Nate, not any man. I stood up, managing to control the trembling in my limbs.

"I got that part," I said casually. "Rehearsals start tomorrow."

"Oh my God!" he said, his face lighting up. "That's amazing!"

"Yeah," I said. "I better get going though. Lots to do. And I need to get home to tell the girls."

I saw his face fall, but I couldn't let myself worry about it. I knew what I was doing.

"Well," he said, smiling again. "I want to take you out to celebrate. This is really amazing."

I shook my head. "I don't know, Nate. I mean, I'm gonna be really busy. This is a huge deal for me, you know?"

"Annie," he said uncertainly. "What's going on? Why are...why are you blowing me off?"

I plastered a look of surprise on my face. "I'm not blowing you off," I said. "I mean, it's not like we're in some serious relationship, right? Wasn't this all supposed to be just a bit of fun?"

"Fun," he said, his voice suddenly tight. "Yeah. Fun."

I chanced a glance at his face and regretted it almost immediately. He looked so sad, so disappointed. I forced it from my mind. I had gone too far with him already, way too far. If I didn't end this now, he would just do it soon himself. I knew that. It was the way it always worked.

"Look, I'll give you a call, okay?" I asked, struggling to keep my voice light.

"Okay," he said. "Sure. Whatever."

I slipped around him and headed down the hall to the front room. I found my purse and put my shoes on, then paused for a moment, waiting for him to come back out. He never did. "See you around, Nate," I finally said, softly, before I left his house.

Chapter Fifteen

I spent the next eighteen hours feeling incredibly annoyed. While I should have been bouncing off the walls in excitement over the show, I instead found that I couldn't keep my mind off of Nate. I had clearly hurt his feelings and that didn't sit well with me. I tried to remind myself that it was no big deal, that I had been clear about what I wanted in Vegas and he had no reason to be upset that I had stuck to it. But for whatever reason, I still felt bad.

"Maybe you miss him," Jen suggested, when I confided this to her over the phone the next day. "Maybe you're feeling bad because you wish you would have stayed there last night and let him celebrate with you."

"I doubt it," I said. "I left because I wanted to."

"Are you sure?"

"What's that supposed to mean?" I snapped, feeling my irritation peak.

"It means that I think you left because you thought you should, not because you wanted to. I think you left because you got scared."

"What in the hell would I have to be scared of?" I asked, feeling stung.

"That you might actually be falling for someone," she said.

"That's ridiculous," I told her. "We barely know each other."

Jen didn't reply. I could tell she didn't believe me and wasn't about to validate my lie with an argument. It was classic Jen—taking the high road and making me feel like a baby in the process.

"Anyhow," I said, determined to change the subject. "How's your day? What're you guys working on?"

"I was actually doing some prep for the benefit," she said. "Getting together a final guest list."

The benefit. Wow. I had totally forgot all about it. Between Nate and the audition, it had slipped my mind entirely.

"That's great," I said. "Thanks again for doing this, Jen."

"No problem," she said. "It's for a good cause. Besides, things are a little slow right now."

I winced. The fall was kind of a scary season for an event planner. Most of the weddings had tapered off and it would be a few weeks still before the holiday planning would start. I was so proud of Jen, leaving her firm to start her own company. It had taken major guts and I wanted nothing more than for her to be successful.

"Do you want me to see if we can raise the budget a little?" I asked.

"No, sweetie, we're fine. Seriously. Don't worry about it. We did great with the wedding season; it will get us through until the holidays pick up. Besides, Kiki's dad always throws some big event our way when he's worried we're too slow."

"Ah, the joys of nepotism," I said.

I was only joking, but Jen sighed. "It does feel a little shady, to tell you the truth."

"Don't be ridiculous," I told her firmly. "Mr. Barker knows how good you are at your job. He loved

Rachel Schurig

what you did for the wedding, remember? I bet he would use you even if you weren't working with Kiki."

"He did give me an amazing recommendation before I left my old job," Jen said, her voice brighter.

"You could feel guilty if you took advantage of him," I said. "If you took his work and did a half-assed job just because he's connected to your partner. But I doubt you would ever do that."

"Of course I wouldn't!" she said, sounding like the very idea offended her. I grinned. I had never met anyone with a work ethic like Jen's.

"Then I don't think you have anything to worry about," I told her. "You earn the money for those jobs."

"Damn right I do," she said. "Okay, enough about that. How are you feeling about the rehearsal?"

When I had arrived home from Nate's last night and told Jen about my part, she had been ecstatic for me. She had immediately called Ginny and demanded she come over so the three of us could celebrate. We drank a bottle of champagne that Jen had been saving for a client and toasted to the beginning of my long and successful career as a paid actress.

"I'm excited," I told her, feeling a thrill in my stomach at the thought. "But a little nervous, too."

"You'll be fine," she assured me. "Seriously, you won that part over a ton of actresses. You need to walk in there with some swagger."

"Go all diva on them?" I asked, smiling.

Jen laughed. "No. But be confident and sure of yourself. You're going to kick ass."

"Thanks, hon," I said.

"Shoot," she said. "The other line is beeping. Want me to call you back?"

"No, I have some work I should be doing," I said, looking down at the piles of paper on my desk. "I'll see you after rehearsal."

"Okay, hon. Break a leg!"

After we hung up I spent several minutes staring at my papers, trying to come up with the motivation needed to get started. It wasn't going to happen. With a surreptitious look over my shoulder to ensure that I was still alone in the office, I pulled my audition materials out of my bag and started reading over the pages I had been given for the callback. Within minutes, I was happily lost in the world of my play.

Chapter Sixteen

*'It's very important, in the early days of your relationship, to keep your options open. I'm not recommending that you date more than one man at the same time, but I also wouldn't recommend that you get so caught up in someone that you close your eyes to other opportunities. You simply never know when or where your soul-mate might arrive.'—**The Single Girl's Guide to Finding True Love***

Pulling up outside of the bar that would be our rehearsal space for the next week, I tried to remember what Jen had told me about confidence. It was not something I normally had an issue with; overbearing was usually a more apt description for me. But this was different. Inside the private room upstairs that Collins had reserved for us were serious professional actors. People who had worked in Chicago and New York. Freaking Jenner Collins, a movie star.

They wanted you for this part, I told myself. *Over any other more established actress. They picked you.*

The pep talk calmed me down a little and I got out of the car, determined to show a little of the swagger that Jen had recommended.

I made my way to the private room above the bar, hearing a babble of noises already. I straightened my faded old Ramones t-shirt (a good luck charm I'd had ever since high school), took a deep breath, and walked in.

There were about six or seven people already gathered inside, making small talk. I recognized a few of them from my callback. The room was on the small side, paneled in dark wood with low-hanging beams. It had an old world pub feel to it that I immediately liked. I made a mental note to bring the girls back here sometime to hang out, before I turned my attention to the group of people standing in the middle of the room.

It appeared as if some of the other actors knew each other, but there were a few people looking about as awkward as I felt. I approached the group with a smile on my face.

"Hey," I said, as everyone turned to look at me. "I'm Annie."

"Hey, Annie," said a good-looking older guy with distinguished graying hair. I immediately recognized him from my callback, as we had read together several times. "I think you're my daughter."

Everyone laughed at this, and I smiled. "Awesome," I said.

A very pretty brunette about my age was glaring at me from the edge of the group. I ignored her, used to this kind of obvious loathing. Even in college it had been rampant in the theater department. Actresses were, by nature, jealous beings.

"Hey, Annie," a voice said from just next to my ear. "I'm Tyler."

I looked over and saw a very cute guy standing right next to me—a little too close, to be honest. He was tall and somewhat thin, with shaggy dark hair and what Jen would refer to as 'designer stubble'. He was attractive, in that creative-type way. I remembered him from my audition as well. This was the guy I had felt such a spark of chemistry with.

"Hi," I said, feeling my heart rate quicken a little. He was giving me a very obvious once over, and the little smile never left his face.

"I think we fall in love," he said softly, his smile turning more smirk-like. I stared at him, not knowing how to respond. "In the show," he clarified, grinning bigger. I had the feeling that he was enjoying making me feel a little uncomfortable.

I grinned back. "Lucky you," I said in my most above-it-all voice. Two could play at that game.

Before he could respond, there were voices on the stairs behind us and everyone turned to look as Jenner Collins entered the room, followed by the tall skinny man I knew to be Jackson Coles, and a woman dressed head-to-toe in black, including a flowing cape sweater thing. From the cape to her severe bun and black rimmed glasses, she had 'artist' written all over her.

"Hey!" Jenner said, in his easy, comfortable way. "I'm so glad you guys are all here!"

Everyone said hello while a few of the braver (or more conceited) amongst us went over to shake his hand. I overheard quite a bit of ass-kissing going on over there, and I struggled not to roll my eyes.

"It's kind of gross, isn't it?" Tyler said, still standing next to me. "Look at how they all throw themselves at him."

I shrugged. "I guess it's part of the game, isn't it?"

"True. Don't think I'm above it. But I'd rather wait for a more intimate time to make my mark." His words dripped with double meaning as his gaze dropped down to my lips, and this time I did roll my eyes.

"So, let's get all the actor measuring-stick bullshit out of the way now," he said.

"What are you talking about?"

"You know. Every time people like us get together we follow the same song and dance. One of us casually mentions a show we worked on and everyone else spends the next ten minutes looking for a way to nonchalantly one-up each other."

I had to laugh at that. It was very true. I couldn't count the number of times I had sat waiting for an audition overhearing that exact conversation. The name-dropping and backhanded bragging that went on when actors got together was a given.

"Not a lot of bragging to do here," I said. "Unfortunately I haven't had many big roles since college."

"Interesting," he said. "A modest one. We don't see too many of your kind in these places, Annie. Hmm, maybe you're waiting to brag about your college experience. Okay, I'll play along. Where did you go to school?"

I laughed again, already liking him a little better than I had a few minutes ago. "I went to Wayne State."

He raised his eyebrows. "So you performed at the Bonstelle Theater, huh? Certainly nothing to be ashamed of. So what shows did you do down there?"

I arranged my features in the faux-modest expression I had seen on countless girls in this situation. "My two most challenging roles were Celia in *As You Like It* and Alma Rose in Arthur Miller's *Playing for Time*."

"I am duly impressed. Now I'll tell you that I went to Northwestern and got my MFA and was slogging away in the pitiless Chicago scene until I was accepted as an intern at the Purple Rose."

"Wow," I said. "That's pretty amazing." I was being totally honest with him: not only was

Northwestern a really great school, but interning at the Purple Rose Theater was a seriously big deal. It was a small company located in Chelsea, which was pretty far out from the city. But it had been started by another local actor turned Hollywood star. They were constantly putting up amazing new shows and their reputation was top-notch. I would kill to work at a theater like that.

"Thank you," Tyler replied. "Now we've got all that bragging out of our system, we can just relax and have fun. Sound good?"

I laughed. "Sounds perfect."

Before we could say more, Jenner Collins was calling for our attention. Jackson was walking around, handing out full scripts, and I felt a thrill of excitement. There were few things in the world I loved more than reading a new play.

"So tonight we're just going to do a pretty basic read-through," Jenner was saying. "We'll also be talking about your characterizations as we go through. I'd like everyone to be off-book as soon as humanly possible; we're on a short schedule and we don't have much time to mess around."

"Ladies and gentlemen, if you could grab a seat," the cape-lady called out, gesturing to the table in the center of the room.

Tyler followed me over and took the seat to my left. The brunette I had noticed earlier was hovering around near Jenner, clearly waiting to see where he would sit before choosing her own place.

Once we were all settled, Jenner smiled at us. "I'm so excited to get started on this show," he said. "It means a lot to me. A good friend of mine wrote the script, and I can't wait to bring it to life with your help."

It was pretty standard director stuff, but he seemed genuine enough. The brunette was absolutely simpering over him.

"Now, there's some pretty exciting news I need to share with you all. We have an opportunity with this show, and while it might not pan out, I still think it's important to mention it."

You could have heard a pin drop around that table. Every single one of us was leaning towards Jenner slightly, eager to hear what he was going to say.

"There's been some initial interest in taking this show to an off-Broadway run."

If it wouldn't be considered so uncool, I bet every single person at that table would have been screaming and jumping up and down. An off-Broadway run was a huge, huge deal. I knew that a few of Jenner's other shows had made similar jumps, but it was still a very rare thing for any production.

"There are some investors interested in working with us," Jenner said. "The plan, for now, is to run the show in Detroit through Christmas then take it to Chicago early in the New Year."

This made sense. For a regional show to make it to New York it needed support and a lot of good buzz. Chicago was a bigger market then Detroit. If we could get some good reviews there...

"Obviously, no casting decisions beyond the Detroit run have been made," the cape-lady said, reminding us all that there were no guarantees in this business. As if any of us didn't realize that.

"Regardless," Jenner said, "the best thing any of us can do is to work really hard and ensure that this Detroit run is as successful as possible. Now, let me introduce my associates. You may have met them during your various auditions. This—" he gestured to cape lady—"is Tabitha Washington, my associate director. Tabitha will be stepping in on those occasions when I can't be at rehearsal. She might also do some one-on-one character work with you. She's highly regarded in our field and you should consider it a great opportunity to work with her."

Tabitha merely nodded imperiously at us all, and I warded off a little shiver. No matter what Jenner said, this lady looked scary as hell. No way was I looking forward to working with her, one-on-one or otherwise.

"This gentlemen here," Jenner continued, pointing to the skinny guy who had run the callback, "is Jackson, my personal assistant. He'll be helping us with any number of issues during the run of the show. So be nice to him." We all chuckled politely, while Jackson glared around at us, probably thinking of all the additional work we were going to be creating in his life.

"She has a previous engagement tonight, but at our next rehearsal, you'll be meeting our stage manager, Christina Goodwin. She's the best in the area."

There were a lot of murmurs at that. Even I knew who Christina Goodwin was. She had worked *everywhere*. That nervous feeling was starting to return with a vengeance. It was hard not to think that I was out of my league here.

To make matters worse, Jenner decided that we should go around the room and introduce ourselves. Of course, the other actors took this as an opportunity to share the greatest hits of their resume. As one middle-aged woman droned on and on about her experiences doing summer stock with the Berkshire Theater Festival, Tyler kicked me under the table. I suppressed my grin.

Once everyone had had their chance to brag, we got down to the read-through. I had read bits and pieces of the script from the callback materials I had gotten, but not quite enough to get a feel for the quality of the work. Within a few scenes I knew that the play was amazing, totally up my alley. It was emotional and poignant but also funny and satirical. Very, very clever. I felt my unease melting away as I enveloped myself in the story. How had I gotten so lucky to be chosen for this?

After the read-through, Jenner and Tabitha wanted us to talk about our characters—how we saw them, what we thought might be motivating their actions. It was a little scary, having only read the script once, but Jenner's enthusiasm and easy attitude was contagious. Soon I was happily brainstorming with the rest of the cast, my inhibitions forgotten.

All in all, it was a cool first rehearsal. I felt like I was already well on my way to getting to know my character and the script. I no longer felt so intimidated by the other actors; my worry was replaced by excitement. And the idea of possibly taking this show out of Detroit, maybe even to New York...it was the kind of thing that I couldn't even let myself imagine.

After we had said our goodbyes, everyone headed off to their respective cars—except for the brunette girl (whose name, incidentally, was Jasmine), who instead hovered around Jenner as he and his associates gathered their materials and made plans for the following night.

"She's something else, isn't she?" Tyler asked me as we headed down the stairs into the main bar. "I've worked with her before and she's always this way—trying to align herself with the most powerful guy in the room. I can't believe her head didn't explode when she found out she'd be working with Collins."

"Do you know him at all?" I asked, glancing over my shoulder to make sure none of the others were behind us. "Jenner? Is he the type to hook up with a groupie like that?"

"I haven't worked with him, but he doesn't have that kind of reputation, from what I hear."

"Good," I said, holding the door open for Tyler. "I hope he rejects her and she's humiliated."

Tyler laughed. "Wow, you're a lot more competitive than I thought."

"Damn straight," I replied as we walked out into the cool evening air. "Mmm," I said, pausing for a moment on the sidewalk. "I love the smell of fall in the air."

"Me too," Tyler agreed. "It's the perfect time for hanging out and having a beer." He looked at me with raised eyebrows, as if offering an invitation.

"Maybe we could do that sometime," I told him with a smile, effectively shooting him down while still leaving the possibility of changing my mind. It was a favorite tactic of mine in dealing with cute boys that had the potential of being dangerous.

As we reached our cars, Tyler gave me a little smirk. "I'll hold you to that," he said, then turned and was gone.

Chapter Seventeen

"Is there anything else I should be doing?" I asked Jen, looking around at her piles of plastic bags, notebooks, and card stock.

"Nope, I think we should be pretty much set," she said, looking down at her notebook. "Oh, wait, on second thought, would you mind giving me a hand with the guest list? I want to make sure I have everyone important."

Jen and I were sitting in the living room, going through the final preparations for the benefit. She and Kiki had been working on the event for the last several days, and I had a feeling they had already put in more hours than their paltry budget allowed for.

"Okay, read me the names," I said.

As Jen went through the list of guests she had invited, I checked each name against the list Marilyn had given me.

Towards the end of her reading, she got to my personal guests.

"Okay, then we have myself, Matt, Kiki and Eric, Ginny and Josh. Is that all? You didn't invite your mom?"

"No," I said, suppressing a shudder at the thought. I paused for a moment. "So all the significant others are coming too?"

She looked at me in surprise. "Well, yeah. I mean, I thought that was...is that okay?"

"Of course," I said hurriedly. I shouldn't have been surprised. Of course Ginny and Jen and Kiki were going to want to bring their guys along. I just hadn't realized I would be the only single one of my friends.

I checked back through the list and realized that I would probably be the only single one period, even including the other theater employees and the donors.

I sighed a little, and regretted it when Jen heard me. "Seriously, Annie, if you want this to be just a girls thing that's totally fine. I'm sure no one will mind."

"No," I said firmly. "Of course I don't want that. Please. You guys don't need to feel bad for me." She looked at me with slightly raised eyebrows. "I chose this whole single thing, you know?" I told her. "I always have fun at a party, dateless or not."

"I just don't understand why you *are* dateless," she said.

"What do you mean?' I asked.

"I mean Nate, of course!" she said. "Why isn't he coming with you?"

"Jen," I groaned. She had brought up Nate no less than a dozen times in the week since I had last seen him.

"Annie," she mimicked. "I don't get it. I mean, you both clearly like each other. What's the big deal?"

"There is no big deal," I told her. "I'm just busy. You know that I have rehearsals every night."

It was true. Since I had found out I'd been cast in the show, I had been working my butt off. When I wasn't at official rehearsals I was studying my lines. I had even met up with some of the other actors at a coffee house to work on getting off-book.

"You don't have rehearsal the night of the benefit," she said. "So it sounds like the perfect time to see him."

I sighed. She had a point. But after I had blown him off so spectacularly the last time...

"What is it?" she asked, watching my face closely. "I know that expression, Annie. What did you do?"

"I was a little rude to him last time I saw him," I admitted. "I had just found out about the show and I was in a hurry to get home and tell you. I guess I blew him off. He didn't seem too happy about it."

"So call and apologize," she said. Jen always made everything sound so simple.

Before I could respond, there was a sound on the front porch. "You expecting someone?" I asked.

There was really no need to ask. Her entire face had lit up in the way it only did when Matt was around. Sure enough, a second later he was opening the door. I guess he'd taken my advice about not needing to knock.

"Hi, girls," he said pleasantly.

Jen was already up on her feet, rushing forward to hug him as if she hadn't seem him in days, though in fact I had spotted him in my kitchen in his boxer shorts that very morning.

"Hey, Annie," he said, coming over to sit on the couch after they had kissed a million times. "How's it going?"

"Pretty good," I replied. "Jen and I were just going over some of the final details for the benefit."

He scrunched up his nose a little bit. "Do I have to wear a suit to this thing?"

"Of course not," I laughed. "Wear whatever you want."

Jen made a face behind his back that made me think I'd be seeing Matt in a suit no matter what. I hid a smile.

"So what are you guys up to tonight?" I asked, stretching my legs out against the floor. I'd had an early afternoon rehearsal so for once I had a free evening.

"I was gonna make some dinner," Jen said. "Then we were planning to stay in and watch a movie."

"You in?" Matt asked me politely.

Out of the corner of my eye I saw his hand resting lightly on Jen's knee. Something about the casualness, the easiness, of that position made my heart ache a little. Suddenly I had no desire to be in the room with them for a second more.

"I don't think so," I said. "I really want to be off-book for rehearsal tomorrow. I think I'll just shut myself up in my room."

"Are you sure?" Jen asked. "You won't even eat with us?"

"Nah," I said, wondering if I had ever once in my life turned down Jen's amazing cooking. "Save me something?"

"Sure," she said.

I caught her expression and noted that she seemed concerned for me. I shrugged it off and headed to my room. Once there, I lay down on my bed, throwing my hand over my eyes.

What was wrong with me? Since when did I feel jealous of my friends? I was revisited by that same emotion I had when watching Ginny and Josh the day Kiki told us about Vegas. It was strange and I wasn't sure that I liked it.

My mind wandered involuntarily to Nate. I had been missing him this week, in a way that scared me. It was so unlike me to spend so much time thinking about a guy. Then again, it was unlike me to spend so much time with any one guy.

Is that really a bad thing? I wondered. I mean, it wasn't like I wanted to marry him. Would it really be so bad to have a boyfriend? It didn't have to be any huge, serious deal. I thought back to his words our last night in Vegas. *We have fun together. Why can't that fun continue in Detroit?*

Well, why couldn't it? If he could be understanding about my need to rehearse, and to spend time with my friends and Danny, why couldn't I see him sometimes?

That is, if he even wanted to see me. I had been pretty rude to him. Maybe he'd had enough of me. The thought made me feel strangely anxious. Nervous, almost. For some reason I couldn't quite place, I really did not like the idea of Nate being upset with me.

Before I could talk myself out of it, I grabbed my phone and found him in the contacts. While it rang, I held my breath.

"Hello?" he finally said. I felt a rush of relief.

"Hi, Nate," I stammered. "It's uh...it's Annie."

Hearing his voice had done nothing to help with my nerves. What was wrong with me?

"Hey, Annie," he said. His voice wasn't cold, but it wasn't exactly warm, either. It sure didn't sound like he had been dying to hear from me. Damn. Maybe this had been a mistake.

"How have you been?" I asked.

"Pretty good," he replied. "Work's been busy. How about you? How's the play?"

"Really good," I told him. "I've been really bogged down with it."

"But you're enjoying yourself?" he asked, and there was a definite edge to his voice now.

"It's a really good show," I told him. "I feel really lucky to be a part of it. I hope that you'll be able to come see it."

"I'm sure I will," he said, his voice softer now. "So, what's up?"

"Well, I was wondering if you had plans on Friday," I told him, crossing my fingers. "I know it's short notice..."

"I was going to meet some friends for a drink after work," he said, and my heart fell. "But nothing's set in stone..."

"I have this benefit," I said in a rush. "For the theater. A fundraising kind of thing where we honor our donors. It will probably be pretty boring but I wondered if you might want to come with me."

"Wow, you really know how to sell an event, Annie," he said, and I noticed that the slight teasing tone I had become so familiar with was back in his voice. For some reason, it made me feel happy.

"Maybe I should rephrase," I said, laughing a little. "I'm going to this super glamorous, super exciting benefit on Friday and I just happen to have an extra ticket. There will be a ton of really interesting, very cool people there. Including the billionaire Jonathon Barker and his glamorous heiress daughter. If you play your cards right, I might just give that ticket to you."

"Oh my God," he breathed. "Would you really?"

I laughed again, and was pleased to hear his own warm chuckle on the other end of the line.

"Well, *now* you've sold me," he said. "What time is this thrilling event?"

I told him the details. "Want me to meet you there or pick you up?" he asked.

Hmm, meeting there was definitely the safest option. But if we went together maybe the night wouldn't have to end with the benefit. The thought of having Nate stay over sent a little thrill though me.

"Would you mind picking me up?" I asked casually. "If it's not out of your way, that is."

"Nope, you're directly on the way," he replied. "So I'll pick you up at seven?"

"Perfect," I said, smiling broadly.

"I'm glad you called, Annie," he said, his voice softer.

"I'm glad I did, too," I admitted. "And I'm glad you can come with me."

"I'll see you in a few days," he said.

After I hung up my phone, I stretched out on the bed, feeling much better about things.

I pulled out my script, deciding that I may as well do what I had told Jen and get my lines nailed down. As I opened to the first scene, I caught a whiff of the unmistakable smell of Jen's lasagna.

I cursed under my breath, really wishing that I hadn't told her I wouldn't eat with them.

Chapter Eighteen

At 6:45 on Friday night, I stood in the middle of my room in nothing but my bra and underwear. I had been staring at my closet for the past five minutes with no clue what to wear. The fifteen minutes before *that* had been spent trying on various options, all to no avail.

"Damn," I said loudly.

I pulled out my phone and called Ginny. "What's up?" she asked.

"I have no idea what to wear," I told her. "And Jen is already at the theater setting up. Help me!"

"Okay, relax," Ginny said. "Just take a deep breath."

"Nate is going to be here any minute!" I cried. She clearly didn't understand my plight. "And I have nothing to wear!"

"Nate, eh?" she asked, a smugness in her voice that made me want to slap her.

"Shut up, Ginny," I growled. "Just help me, okay?"

This was not typical behavior for me. I usually had no problem picking my clothes because I generally only bought things that I liked. And it wasn't like I was super worried about impressing the donors or the people at work—I mean, I saw most of them every day. So what was wrong with me now?

Nate, a voice in my head said. *You're nervous about seeing him again.*

"Okay," Ginny was saying, and I forced myself to concentrate on what she was saying. "What about that black sweater dress you have?"

"Hmm," I replied, rifling through my clothes to find the garment. "Okay, it's here."

"I think if you paired that with grey tights and those black leather boots Jen has...you know, the slouchy, flat-heeled ones?"

I had a mental image of the boots she was talking about. They were perfect, and would look great with this dress.

"You're a lifesaver," I sighed.

"Wear your red blazer over it for some color," she instructed. "And your silver bangles. You'll look great."

"Ginny McKensie," I told her, "you are amazing and my very best friend."

"Yeah, yeah, yeah," she said. "I bet you'll say the same thing to Jen when she asks you why you're in her boots."

"True," I said, grinning. Just then I heard a knock at the door. "Shit! He's here, gotta go!"

"See you soon," she said, and I hung up.

I pulled the sweater dress on as quickly as I could, careful not to mess up my hair. I had done it in the same soft, braided style that Ginny had recommended in Vegas. At least I wouldn't have to worry about the frizz factor tonight.

I heard Nate knock again.

"Tina!" I bellowed. "Can you get the door?"

There was silence from her bedroom. Awesome. Barefooted, I ran to living room, pulling open the door. Sure enough, Nate was standing there, looking gorgeous in dress pants and a long black wool overcoat.

"Hang on!" I said, before he could even say hello, turning away from the door. "Come on in!" I called over my shoulder as I ran back to my room. I hurriedly pulled on my grey tights, praying I wouldn't run them. Outside the room, I heard Nate coming into the house.

"Sorry," I called out. "Running a little late."

"Take your time," he replied. "I'll just have a little snoop around."

I heard him laugh and I knew he was getting me back for my nosing in his apartment. I better get him out of here quick.

Finishing with my tights, I dashed into Jen's room. Unlike mine, which now looked like a bomb had exploded, Jen's room was neat as a pin. Typical. I pulled open her closet door and saw that all of her shoes were neatly arranged. There were her boots, right in the back.

"Thanks," I muttered, grabbing them. I sat on her bed and pulled them on.

Ginny was a genius. These boots were totally gorgeous, a soft, slouchy black leather. They came up practically to my knees, but the flat heel kept them from looking too sexy. They were the perfect complement to my dress.

Once I had them on and zipped, I ran back into my room to find the jewelry.

"Annie," Nate said. I looked up to find him standing in my doorway. "Relax. We have plenty of time."

The sight of him there, looking so incredibly handsome, only made me feel more flustered.

I caught his eye glancing around my room, at the clothes strewn haphazardly across the bed and dresser. "Uh, sorry about the mess," I muttered.

Nate smiled at me. "Just finish getting ready, okay? Stop worrying."

It would be easier if you weren't standing there staring me, I thought to myself. Nevertheless I dug through my jewelry box until I found the bangles Ginny had recommended. Once I was ready, I grabbed my bottle of rose perfume from the dresser and gave myself a good spritzing. When I was done, I looked up at Nate.

He was still staring at me, but he now had a slight smile on his face. "What?" I asked.

"It smells like you," he replied. "That scent. It smells like you in Vegas."

I blushed a little. This was my favorite perfume, and I had in fact used it in Vegas. It gave me a funny feeling to know that he had remembered it.

"Well," I said, a little awkwardly. "Are you ready?"

"Of course," he said. He held out his hand to me. "Shall we?"

***

Jen and Kiki had done an amazing job on the benefit. The stage and lobby area of the Springwells had totally been transformed. They had scattered high-top tables around the room and hung paper lanterns from the light rigging. The walls and tables were dotted with framed photos of kids participating in events or acting on stage. It looked great.

They had allocated most of the budget to hors d'oeuvres and drinks, even setting up a little bar area serving soft drinks and wine. It was the nicest event we had ever had at our little theater, and I could tell that Marilyn was really pleased. The bitter look stuck on Grayson's face throughout the night was a bonus.

An hour in and I was actually enjoying myself, a first for me at a work event. But then again, I didn't usually have my best friends with me at work events. And I definitely didn't usually have Nate.

I was pleased with how well he got along with my friends. The girls seemed totally taken with him, and it gave me a little feeling of pride to know he had their approval. He also seemed to hit it off with Josh, which was a little surprising to me. I would have thought he had more in common with Matt.

I told him so as we were waiting at the bar for our drinks. "Matt's cool," he said, shrugging.

"It just seems like you're getting along better with Josh," I pressed him.

"Josh is cool too," he replied, shrugging again. I rolled my eyes. Guys never thought about these things in the same way that girls did.

"He told me you guys didn't always see eye to eye," Nate said, taking his wine from the waiter and raising a questioning eyebrow at me.

"That's an understatement," I said, taking my own glass.

"Why?" Nate asked.

"It's kind of a long story," I told him.

"I've got time. And I love some good gossip."

I smiled at him. "Josh and Ginny dated for years," I said in a low voice. He leaned down to hear me better and I shivered a little at his new proximity. "They lived together during college and ended up breaking up right before they graduated."

"Ooh," Nate said. "Scandal."

"You haven't heard the half of it!" I told him. "So Ginny, Jen, and I moved in together in Ferndale. We thought she was trying to get over him, but little did we know they hooked up."

"Uh-oh," Nate said. "I think I see where this is going."

I nodded. "Danny. That's how Ginny got pregnant. But after their hook-up they didn't leave things in a very positive way. So Ginny didn't want to tell him about the baby. By the time she got up the courage, he had changed his number and moved."

"Wow," Nate said. "That's kind of cold."

"Right?" I asked, relieved that he thought so. "Anyhow, things got even crazier. Ginny finally got in touch with Josh's parents and they convinced her that he didn't want anything to do with the baby. They said he knew about it but he didn't want to see her. They even offered her money to stay away."

"This is better than a soap opera!" Nate said, and I laughed.

"Well, the truth finally all came out and Josh found out about the baby. Ginny forgave him and they ended up getting married...but I guess I still held a grudge for a while."

"But if he didn't know about the baby..."

"He still slept with her and then disappeared for almost a year," I pointed out. "I don't like guys who pull shit like that with my friends."

"They mean a lot to you," he said. It was a statement, not a question.

I nodded. "They're my family."

"Sounds like a lot for a guy to compete with," he said, looking over at Josh and Matt, who were both chatting with Mr. Barker.

"Silly Nate," I told him, taking his hand. "There is no competition. There isn't a guy that has a chance."

"We can only hope for second place, huh?" he asked, smiling.

"Third," I said. He looked confused. "Danny. He's the top guy in our lives."

Nate laughed and put his arm around me. "Third isn't so bad," he murmured. "Come on, let's go see your friends."

***

The night was a smashing success. Marilyn complimented me in front of Grayson and thanked me for my hard work. Kiki's father had spent twenty minutes talking with her about opportunities for patronage. He wanted to fund an entire camp. Marilyn was thrilled.

"That was fun," Nate said as we headed toward his car.

"Thank you for coming," I told him. I shivered slightly in the cold and he put his arm around me.

"It's really turning to fall now," he said, looking up at the clear sky.

"I miss Vegas," I sighed.

"Me too," he said, looking down at me. I wondered if he meant the weather or the time that we had spent together there.

We reached the car and he stopped to open the door for me. Ever the gentleman.

"So what's next?" he asked once we were both inside.

"What do you feel like?" I asked him. "I'm a little hungry..."

"Food it is," he agreed, putting the car into drive. "Want to go somewhere?"

At that precise moment, I yawned. He smiled over at me. "Or not. We could always get pizza and head back to my place."

"That sounds perfect," I said.

"Why don't you call and we can pick it up on the way?" he said, pulling his phone from his coat pocket and handing it to me.

"You have a pizza place on your speed dial?" I asked incredulously.

He shrugged. "Sure. I'm a single guy, what do you expect?"

"Says Mr. Foodie," I muttered. I dialed the number and placed an order for a large with everything as Nate drove.

Twenty minutes later he was opening the door to his apartment while I held the piping hot pizza in my hands. "Hurry," I moaned. "I'm starving."

He laughed as he pushed open the door. "Calm down."

"I told you when we first met, I'm a girl with an appetite."

"So you did," he said, taking the pizza from me and setting it on the counter. He pulled down two plates and I got to work dishing out the food. "Beer or soda?" he asked, opening the fridge.

"Hang on," I told him, stopping what I was doing to hold up my hand. "You're in Michigan now, Mister. We don't say soda."

He rolled his eyes. "Excuse me. Would you like a beer or a *pop*?"

I grinned. "Beer, please."

We spread out on the floor of the living room and Nate put some music on his iPod speakers. I listened closely for a minute until I could make out the artist. The Smiths. I was quite impressed with his taste. I would have pegged him as a frat-rock type of guy.

While we ate, he told me all about the project he was working on. I normally found cars to be about the most boring subject on the face of the earth, but Nate was good at telling stories. The way he got so excited about his work was adorable—his eyes got brighter and he blinked a lot. I wondered if I looked that happy when I was talking about theater.

Once we were done with the food, we moved over to the couch. I had an urge to snuggle up to Nate, but I wasn't sure how he would feel about that. He had held my hand a few times at the benefit but he had made no move to kiss me. I wondered if he was still a little mad at me.

"I was surprised to hear from you," he said, and I felt my stomach drop a little. I should have known that he would want to talk about what happened.

"I should have called earlier," I told him. "I was just so busy—"

He held up his hand to stop me. "Listen, Annie. You made it perfectly clear that you weren't looking for anything serious," he said. "I think I probably pressured you a little bit when we first got back, pushing you to see me every day. That was a mistake."

It was strange. Him referring to our time together as a mistake bothered me. A lot.

"I do like you," he said softly, reaching out to take my hand. "And I want to spend time with you. I promise that we'll chill out though, okay?"

I nodded, not really sure how I felt about this. Wasn't he basically telling me exactly what I had wanted to hear?

"But, Annie," he said, holding my gaze seriously. "I'm not interested in games, either. I don't need to be strung along. We can keep things casual but if it's going to be all hot and cold with you, then I'm sorry, I'm not interested."

"I understand," I said, squeezing his hand. "I'm...I'm sorry if it felt that way to you. I just...I think

I got scared." I sighed and ran my free hand through my hair. "God, listen to me. I'm really not good at this kind of thing." I had a sudden urge to tell him that I avoided these types of conversations like the plague. That I'd never really had a real boyfriend before. Is that what he was going to become?

"You're doing fine," Nate said. "We'll just take it slow, okay? No pressure."

"No pressure," I repeated.

"So, having said all that..." Nate grinned at me mischievously. "Wanna spend the night?"

I smiled back, and leaned forward for a kiss.

"Thought you'd never ask."

Chapter Nineteen

"I swear to God, Jen, I'm just gonna quit," I fumed, throwing open the cabinet door so hard that it slammed into the wall. "I just don't think I can take it anymore!"

"You're stressed," Jen soothed. "There's a lot going on. Let's go sit down and relax."

It was three weeks after the benefit and only a week before the show was set to open. I was definitely starting to feel the strain, and to top it off, I'd had a horrible fight with Grayson at the end of the day. He had insinuated that I was devoting to much of myself to the play, and not enough to my job. Which was completely ridiculous. I worked my ass off for those kids and he took all the credit. I felt my anger rise all over again at the memory of it.

"How the hell am I supposed to relax?" I asked Jen. I immediately felt bad for snapping at her, but she didn't mention it. "The show opens in a week," I said, more calmly. "I'm scared out of my mind. And now all of this from that little jerk..."

Suddenly I felt tears spring to my eyes. Jen raised her eyebrows in surprise. "That's it," she said. "Couch, now. I'll get the wine, you just go sit down."

I listened to her orders without complaint, feeling a little surprised by my own reaction. I usually dealt with stress much better than this. It was not like me to burst into tears over a little confrontation with Grayson.

Jen met me on the couch a few minutes later with two full glasses of merlot. She handed me one and pulled my feet up into her lap. "Just relax," she said, patting my legs gently.

I leaned back into the cushions and closed my eyes, breathing deeply for a few minutes. When I was sure that the weepiness had passed, I opened my eyes and took a drink of my wine.

"Little better?" Jen asked.

"Yeah, thanks," I told her. "Sorry. I don't know what got into me."

"You're under a lot of stress," Jen told me. "This show is a huge deal for you. It's normal to freak a little. Believe me, I've been there."

She had a point. It was only a year ago that Jen had practically had a breakdown overworking herself for Kiki's wedding. If anyone understood about work stress, it was her.

"I just don't think I can handle working at Springwells anymore," I told her. "Seriously, Jen. It makes me crazy every day. I like the kids, I like planning activities for them and working with them. I think the theater is great for the neighborhood. ButI'm so tired of doing paperwork all day. And Grayson...why does he have to make everything so hard?"

"Some people are just like that," Jen said. "You can't change them and you can't tear yourself up trying to please them."

"I know," I said, taking another sip of wine. "It's just really hard when you have to work with them."

"You're so close, Annie," she told me. "You know that, don't you? This show is going to do well, I can just feel it. And think of how it will look on your resume. You're going to start getting more work. Maybe it's time to ditch the day job."

I shook my head. "Even with what we're making for this show there's no way I could afford rent if I quit my job."

"I actually wanted to talk to you about that," Jen said. "Tina's sublease is up in two weeks. I've talked to her and she said she doesn't plan on renewing."

"Shit," I said. I wouldn't miss her at all, but in the mad rush of prepping the show I had completely forgotten that we needed to look for another roommate. "We need to get an ad in the paper!"

Jen held up her hand. "Hear me out first. And please know that you can say no, okay? There's no pressure here."

I looked at her, feeling confused.

"I want Matt to move in."

I felt my stomach lurch and I had to set down my wine glass. I was so not expecting that.

"It's just...I feel like we're ready to move on to the next step, you know?" I appreciated that Jen kept her eyes locked on mine, not lowering her gaze or acting like she was embarrassed...like she pitied me.

"But I'm also not ready to move out. And I'm certainly not ready to stop living with you." She reached out and took my hand. "I mean that, Annie. I still miss having Gin around every day. There's no way I'm ready for us to be split up too."

I felt my heart rate slow down a little bit. So she wasn't asking me to move out...

"You know how Matt is all into real estate," she went on. "He would never, ever be okay with renting."

Matt owned his own construction firm. In the past few months he had been expanding more into development, buying some of the properties his crew fixed up instead of just working for developers.

"He says with the market the way it is right now, it would be a great time for him to buy a house."

"He wants to buy this place?" I asked.

Jen nodded. "Then he could spend the next few years putting some work into it. Fixing up the kitchen, maybe finishing the basement. By the time we're ready to move on the value will have gone up by quite a bit. It's a smart business move."

"So you and I would live here and pay him rent?" I asked. The idea made me feel weird.

"We'd contribute to the mortgage, yeah," she said. "But the great thing is that it'd be much cheaper. Our landlord is gouging us right now. At today's prices, Matt's mortgage would be about two thirds of what we pay now in rent."

She looked so excited discussing these business matters. Jen was definitely a nerd when it came to stuff like this. And I could see her point—it would make financial sense for Matt to own the property. If it lowered our rent that would only be a good thing.

But living in Matt's house? Living with Matt and Jen? It made me uncomfortable, even though I couldn't put my objections into words. It just felt funny. Granted, Matt was here almost every night anyhow, he practically already lived with us. But still...

"Just think about it, okay?" Jen said. "I think it would be really great, but it's up to you."

"I'll think about it," I promised.

"Matt will be here tonight if you have any questions," she continued. I could tell she was excited about the whole thing, and I felt a little bad for my reservations.

"I think I'm going to see Nate after rehearsal," I told her.

"That's almost every night this week, isn't it?" she asked, the forced casualness in her voice not lost on me. I had the feeling she was dying to ask me to dish about my relationship but was trying to restrain herself.

I wasn't quite sure what I would tell her if she did ask. I had been seeing an awful lot of Nate since the benefit. The truth was, we were having a great time. He was easy to be with, he was fun, he made me laugh. If I was any other girl I'd probably be trying to come up with ways to get my claws into him for good.

But in spite of all those good things, something was holding me back. I just wasn't sure how far I wanted to take it. I had an urge to tell Jen all of this, to ask her what I should do. But then again, she would probably just advocate for me to get serious with him. Jen made no secret of her opinion that I was only single because I was repressing issues about my dad's abandonment. Whatever that meant.

"I probably won't get to see him much in the next week," I told her instead. "What with tech and all."

Tech week was my least favorite part of doing a show. During the week before the opening we would have dress rehearsal every day, a chance to run the entire show with all the technical aspects. By the end of the week everything should be pretty smooth, but the first few rehearsals would be rife with bugs. It was just about guaranteed. And that meant long nights trying to work everything out...

"When does tech start?" Jen asked.

"Tomorrow. We're going to run twice. I'll probably be at the theater all day." Not the most exciting way to spend a Saturday.

"So tonight's the last night to see the boy before all the craziness starts?" she asked with a smile. I rolled my eyes. "And then Friday is the opening?"

"We have a press preview on Thursday," I said, my stomach twisting at the thought. "Then official opening is Friday, yeah."

"And you reserved our tickets?" she asked.

"Yup, you guys are all set. Good thing, too, because we're totally sold out."

Jen gasped. "Oh my God, hon, that's amazing!"

"And scary."

"Don't be silly," she said. "You're going to be great."

"I hope so," I told her. "We all need to be great if we want to get this play to Chicago."

Jen's face clouded a little. "I'll be so sad when you're gone," she said.

"It's a long shot."

Jen only shook her head. "Nope. This thing is going all the way. I can feel it."

I smiled at her. I didn't say it, but I had a feeling she was right.

***

Four hours later and I was finally leaving rehearsal. Our final run before tech had gone really well. My frustration over Grayson and work had evaporated under the exhilaration that came from a good rehearsal. When I got to Nate's house, I was practically bouncing off the walls.

"Good rehearsal?" he asked with a smile.

"Awesome rehearsal," I corrected. "God, theater is amazing. Seriously. The next time I complain about something, remind me how good I feel right now."

He came over to put his arms around me and I met him with an enthusiastic kiss.

"We should go out and do something fun," he said, smiling down at me. "Let's not waste this good mood."

He took me to club in Ferndale so we could dance. Most of the guys I knew would drop dead before they would be seen out on a dance floor—not Nate. He seemed to have no inhibitions about looking ridiculous, as long as he was having fun.

The DJ mostly featured hits from the seventies and eighties, so the club lacked that competitive feel you got in many places. In fact, most of our fellow revelers were quite a bit older than us.

"This place is hilarious," Nate said at the bar. We had finally taken a break to get drinks and we were now happily watching the crowd dance. "Do you see that old dude in bellbottoms?"

"He's reliving his youth," I told him. "I think it's awesome."

"You mean groovy," he corrected, putting his arm around me. I was sweaty and disheveled from all of the dancing, but I didn't care. From the way he pulled me closer, I could tell that Nate didn't care either.

"Ready to get back out there?" I asked.

"I'd rather get you home," he said in my ear.

"We've only been here for an hour!" I laughed.

"I don't care. You're gorgeous," he said, his voice low. Even after all these weeks it still sent a thrill through me when he talked like that. I looked up into his eyes, which were dark and intense.

"Okay," I said, happiness filling me up right down to my toes. "Let's go home."

***

An hour later, I was curled up comfortably in Nate's bed, trying to keep him from falling asleep.

"Talk to me," I told him, slapping his chest. "Come on, I need entertainment."

"You're a spoiled child," he moaned, throwing his arm over his face. "I'm tired."

"You're no fun," I shot back. "How old are you?"

"I don't understand how you're not sleepy yet," he said, rolling over so he was facing me. "You had to go into work this morning, you had rehearsal, we went dancing, I just totally ravished you..."

I laughed. "Maybe your ravishing skills aren't as effective as you thought."

He raised an eyebrow at me. "Don't make me show you again."

"I thought you were so tired," I teased, rolling away from him and swinging my legs over the bed. "I'm going to get a drink. Want anything?"

"Nah, I'll just admire the view," he said.

I rolled my eyes and headed to his dresser. I had no desire to put my sweaty dance clothes back on. I rummaged through a drawer until I found a worn gray t-shirt. Pulling it over my head, I smiled a little; it smelled like Nate.

"You just help yourself there, Ann," he called over from the bed.

"Thanks, I will," I told him sweetly.

I headed out to the kitchen, grabbing a glass from the cabinet, then pulling a pitcher of water from the fridge. The clock on the stove blinked one a.m. I thought of Nate, surely falling asleep in bed, but felt too keyed up to join him just yet. Instead, I found my purse and pulled my iPod out, plugging it into his docking stereo. I hit shuffle and smiled as the strains of Billie Holiday filled the living room.

I wandered over to his bookshelf, thinking I might read until I calmed down a bit. On the bottom shelf he had a stack of board games and a few decks of cards.

"Whatcha doing?"

I looked up and saw Nate standing in the doorway in his boxer shorts. He still looked sleepy, but he was smiling at me.

"I thought I might play some cards," I said.

Nate snorted. "You can't play cards. I was in Vegas with you, remember?"

"I can play solitaire," I said in my best 'so-there' voice.

"How about we play something else?" he suggested, coming over to join me. "I have some games."

"Yeah, I was looking at your games," I said with a smirk. "Star Wars Risk, eh? Not at all dorky there, Hughes."

"Oh, shut up," he said, tweaking my ear. "What do you feel like?"

"Monopoly," I said immediately. I loved Monopoly.

"Oh, God," he muttered, pulling it from the shelf. "It's the longest game in the world. We're gonna be up all night."

We settled down at the kitchen table. Nate insisted that I sit on his lap. "If you're going to make me stay up, I better at least get something out of it."

I complied. To be honest, I loved the feel of leaning back against his chest, though I would never admit it to anyone. A month ago if you would have told me that I'd be willing to sit on a guy's lap, I would have laughed in your face.

We played for a few minutes. I insisted that Nate be the car, to go with his job, and I took the dog.

"We used to have a Scottie dog just like this, when I was little," I told him. "Taffy. She was the best dog."

"What happened to her?" he asked, rolling the dice.

"She died. When I was eight." I frowned a little at the memory. Taffy had gotten cancer, and we had to put her down.

I had a sudden clear memory of lying in my bed late at night, terrified and wishing Taffy was there. She usually slept on the foot of my bed, and somehow it always made me feel less scared when my dad wasn't around. He had been gone when she died.

"Annie," Nate said in my ear. "You there?"

I looked over at him, trying to clear my head. "What?" I asked.

"You went away for a minute there. You okay?"

"Yeah," I told him. "Sorry. Maybe I'm sleepier than I thought."

"We could always go to bed," he asked hopefully.

"Not a chance, mister. I plan to beat you at this game."

We settled into the game for a while. I had already amassed Kentucky and Indiana, as well as all of the pink properties. Nate had three of the four railroads as well as Park Place. He teased me constantly throughout the game, questioning my choices and encouraging me to give up my own properties and move in with him in the luxury penthouse he planned to build on Park Place.

"What the hell are we listening to?" he asked suddenly.

I paused for a minute so I could hear. Crap. I had forgotten this was on here.

"Uh, this would be the original Broadway cast of *Pippin*," I admitted.

"You have this on your iPod?" he asked. I could hear the amusement in his voice.

"Yes," I said with dignity.

"Get up," he said, smacking me lightly on the ass.

"Hey!" I cried, but he was already slipping out from under me and heading to the stereo. "What are you doing?"

"I just want to see what else is on here," he said.

"Nate, don't."

"Why? You're always criticizing everyone else's music tastes." He had a bit of a point there—I did tend to be a snob about music. "Don't you have to balls to back up your mouth?"

I glared at him, but didn't argue anymore.

"Wow," Nate said. "Original Broadway cast of *Rent*. And I see we have *Oklahoma...Evita. Cats,* Annie? Really?"

"Shut up," I said in a small voice. "That show ran on Broadway for eighteen years."

"Yeah, but to have it on your iPod?" he said, laughing. "Remember earlier when you called me a dork for having a *Star Wars* game?"

"Betty Buckley was in that show," I muttered, mostly to myself.

"Yeah, don't know who that is," he said, continuing to scroll through my music. "Ah, here we go." He pressed a button and I heard the opening strains of *Edelweiss*, from *The Sound of Music*. "My mom loved this song," he said. "She used to sing it while she cleaned the bathroom."

"It is a pretty good song," I agreed.

"Come here," he said, holding out his arms. I went to him and he pulled me close, beginning to dance.

"Slow dancing in the living room?" I said, looking up at him as he slowly swayed me around the room. "Who's dorky now?"

"Shut up, Annie," he said, kissing me softly. "Just shut up and dance with me."

Chapter Twenty

"Ginny," I said into my phone. "Are you guys here yet?"

"What's wrong?" she asked immediately.

"I think I'm having a panic attack," I told her. "Where are you guys?"

"I just walked into the lobby," she said. "Doesn't look like Jen's here yet."

"Will you come back?" I asked her. "Please, Gin. I really need to see you."

"Just tell me where to go."

I gave her instructions then sat at my dressing table, nervously twisting my hands and trying not to burst into tears. After four weeks of rushed rehearsals, opening night was finally upon me. I had been fine all day, excited even, but as soon as my dressing room partner Mary had finished getting ready and left the room, I felt like I might die.

There was a knock on my door and I looked up to see Ginny standing there. "Oh, Ann," she said. "You look gorgeous."

My costume was simple. As I was playing a college aged girl in modern times, I was dressed in wide-legged black pants and a white, baggy sweater. My hair had been straightened then re-curled in soft waves around my face.

"Seriously," Ginny said, approaching my table. "You look lovely."

"I think I'm going to throw up," I told her seriously.

"You're not," Ginny soothed, patting my shoulder. "Just relax."

"Is it full out there?" I asked her. "I mean, does it look like a lot of people?"

"It's pretty full," she told me. I whimpered a little.

"Come on," she said firmly. "This is silly. You're Annie Duncan, for God's sake. You don't get worked up over a couple people in a theater. Remember that show you did at Wayne, the Shakespeare? That crowd was much bigger than this one. And I didn't hear you freaking out before that."

"Yeah, but this is real," I said. "That was a student production. This is *Jenner Collins's* show. There are investors out there."

"I understand that," Ginny said patiently. "But that shouldn't matter to your performance."

I took a deep breath. "You're right," I said. "You're right. This is going to be fine."

"So, where's Nate sitting?" she asked, changing the subject. "Did you put him by us?"

"Uh, no, actually," I said, feeling my stomach clench for an entirely different reason. "Nate isn't coming tonight."

Ginny raised her eyebrow at me. "Why?"

"I told him not to. I want a couple shows under our belt before he sees it."

She didn't say anything and I knew she didn't really believe me. The truth was, Nate and I had had a bit of a fight over the subject of my opening night. He had wanted to be here and wasn't too happy when I told him I'd rather he wait.

"It will be a better show if you give it a week," I told him.

"I don't care about that," he said impatiently. "Opening night is a big deal. And I want to be there for you."

Yeah, that's exactly what I'm worried about. When I didn't say anything, he sighed. "Are we back here again, Annie? More games?"

"No," I said, feeling exasperated. "Jesus, Nate. I just would rather you see it after we're a bit more comfortable. Besides, the girls are all coming on opening night. I'll have support then. If you come to a different show it'll be like spreading the support out, you know?"

He didn't say anything for a minute. I had a feeling he was trying to keep himself from flipping out on me. "Fine," he said at last. "Whatever you want, Annie."

Now that opening night was upon me, I was really regretting that decision. Why hadn't I just asked him to come? I hated to admit it, but it would make me feel a lot better to know that he was in the audience.

"I should probably get out there," Ginny said, looking down at her watch. "Jen should be here by now."

I felt another rush of nerves, but pushed it down so I could give her a hug. "Thanks for coming back and talking me down," I told her.

"No problem, Ann," she said, squeezing me tight. "Break a leg."

She looked me square in the face and I was surprised to see her eyes had grown wet. "I'm so proud of you," she whispered.

"You haven't even seen it yet," I laughed. "You might hate it."

"Won't matter," she said. "I'll still be proud of you."

After she left I stared at myself in the mirror for a few minutes. Curtain opened in fifteen minutes. I wasn't in the first scene, so I still had a little time. I touched up my lipstick and fiddled with my hair a little. Not much to do now but wait.

"Annie?" said a voice from the doorway. I turned and saw the assistant house manager holding a huge bouquet of red roses. "These just came for you," she said. "And Jenner wants everyone gathered in the greenroom in five."

"Thanks, Jane," I told her, taking the flowers from her hands.

I was expecting the girls, so I got a little shock when I saw Nate's distinctive handwriting on the card.

'I know you wanted me to wait, but I came anyways. Hope you're not too mad. Just wanted to be here. Break a leg.'

I felt my throat well up a little. Nate. He was here. For some reason the thought made me exceedingly happy. I went over and set the flowers on my dressing table, then headed out to meet the cast in the greenroom. My nerves had faded to a low background hum. I felt better than I'd felt all night.

***

The show went about as well as I could have hoped for. There were a few slipups, mostly with cues, but the girls assured me that they hadn't even noticed.

"You were fantastic," Jen said, wiping her eyes. "Seriously, Ann. I loved it."

"She cried the whole time," Matt muttered, and Jen elbowed him in the ribs.

"I was a bit weepy myself," Ginny admitted, pulling me in for a hug. "Didn't I tell you it would be amazing?"

I smiled at her, but I couldn't help peering surreptitiously over her shoulder. I hadn't seen Nate yet.

"He's behind you," Josh said drily.

I spun around, and sure enough, Nate was striding across the lobby toward me. I couldn't have held the grin off my face if I tried. Instead, I threw my arms around his neck and he pulled me close. Out of the corner of my eye, I thought I saw Ginny and Jen give each other a knowing smile, but I was too happy to care.

"You were amazing," he said in my ear. "I'm so proud of you."

"I'm glad you came," I said. "Thank you for the flowers."

I pulled back and smiled goofily at him. Josh's smirking face finally snapped me out of it, and I pulled myself together. "So, what does everyone feel like doing?"

"Don't you want to go out with the cast?" Ginny asked.

"Nope. I've been with them all week and I haven't seen you guys in ages. I'm sure there'll be plenty of cast parties before this thing is over. Tonight I want to see you."

It was true. Though we'd talked on the phone a few times, I hadn't seen Nate since the night we had danced in his living room. Tech week had simply taken up all of my time. And it was a rare occasion for Ginny and Josh to have a sitter for Danny that wasn't me or Jen. I figured we'd better take advantage of it.

We decided on a brewery down the street from the theater. It was close enough to walk, and I was secretly happy to stroll down the street with Nate's arm wrapped around me.

"It's really getting cold," he muttered. "How did fall go by so fast?"

"I feel like I missed it," I told him.

"Well you were holed up in a theater for most of the past month," he agreed. "We'll have to make the most of winter. Do you like to ski?"

"I've never tried it," I told him. "But I'm not really into sporty things like that."

Nate only sighed. "Time to open your horizons a little."

As we all sat down in the restaurant, I had a feeling that I already had. It was very rare for the girls and I to all have a guy in our life at the same time. I couldn't remember many times where the three of us had been on a triple date like this. It felt kind of nice.

We ordered beer and burgers. Nerves had kept me from being able to eat much throughout the day, so I was pretty hungry. Nate was nice enough to let me finish his fries.

"You're such a brat," Ginny said, watching me eat. "You eat like that all the time and you never put on any weight."

Jen and I immediately burst out laughing. Ginny was drop-dead gorgeous. Like, seriously, she could have been a model if she wasn't so short.

"I'm serious!" she said. "Ever since Danny I put on weight if I even look at this kind of food."

"Oh my God," I said. "I was there when you picked out your wedding dress, remember? I know what size it was. And I sure as hell wouldn't fit into it."

"Are we really talking about weight and clothes?" Matt asked. "I mean, it's fine if we are. Just let me know so I can zone out."

"Oh, shut up," Jen said. "We're allowed to be girly every once in a while."

However, she did change the subject. "So tell me about the cast," she said. "Now that I know faces to match the names to."

"That brunette, who played Mia? She's a total bitch," I said, and they all laughed. "Seriously. Her name is Jasmine and she glares at me every time we're in the same room together. She also throws herself at Jenner every chance she gets. It's totally disgusting."

"Who was your boyfriend?" Jen asked. "That guy was pretty cute. I'm surprised you never mentioned him."

A slight blush came to my cheeks, and I felt Nate's eyes on my face. Tyler had continued to be very flirty with me, but I had never taken him up on his offer to get beer. I had never told the girls about him though, because I knew they would think he was just the kind of guy that I usually went for.

"That was Tyler," I said. "He's kind of a—"

"Better watch what you say, Miss Duncan," a voice from behind me said. I turned in my chair and found myself looking up at Tyler himself.

"Hey," I said, laughing to cover my awkwardness. "How's it going?"

"Pretty good," he said. "I'm meeting a few friends here."

He looked around at my group and I realized I should probably introduce him. "Tyler, these are my friends. Guys, this is Tyler."

"Her boyfriend," he added. "In the show, I mean." He did that smirking thing again and I felt myself grow annoyed. Then I felt Nate's hand come to rest lightly on the back of my neck. Tyler's smirk grew.

"Well, nice to meet you all," he said. "See you tomorrow, Annie."

As soon as he was gone, Nate dropped his hand. "What the hell was that?" I asked him quietly, so the others wouldn't hear.

"What?"

"That whole possessive bullshit."

"I wasn't being possessive," he said, but he didn't meet my eyes.

"Right. You just happened to put your hand on me at the precise moment that guy was being flirty. There was no message in that at all."

"Sorry," he said, looking up at me. "I just didn't like him, okay? I don't like how he looks at you."

I rolled my eyes. "Tyler is an ass," I told him. "But I don't need that kind of shit from you, okay?"

"Fine," he said, sounding pissed. "I didn't even realize I was doing it. Sorry."

The rest of our meal felt a little strained after that. Stupid Tyler, having to ruin everything.

And Nate, I thought to myself. Acting like a jealous, possessive guy. Isn't that exactly why I never wanted a boyfriend? Didn't they all turn out this way?

Chapter Twenty-one

The following night I decided to go out with the cast after the show. Everyone was planning to head over to a bar in midtown that Jenner co-owned. He had promised that our drinks would be on the house.

The bar was really nice, though a little swanky for my taste. I noticed that Jasmine seemed to be perfectly in her element. After we arrived, I watched her for a minute. She was still throwing herself shamelessly at Jenner, always standing close to him, touching his arm when she was talking, thrusting her chest out whenever she had his attention. It was nauseating. At least he didn't seem to be at all affected by it. Maybe there was hope for the male species after all.

"So, you decided to join us tonight," Tyler said, sliding up to me at the bar. "Whatcha drinking?"

"Newcastle," I responded, avoiding making eye contact.

"Nice," he said. "I had you pegged for a fruity cocktail kind of girl."

"Guess you don't know me so well," I said.

"You're pissed at me," he said suddenly, smiling like he thought the realization was amusing.

"Why would I be pissed at you?" I asked him. "I barely know you."

"You didn't like me talking to you last night in front of your boyfriend."

I turned to him, feeling annoyed. "Okay, first of all, you can talk to whoever you want. I couldn't care less what you do. Second, he isn't my boyfriend. He's just a guy I'm dating. And none of this is any of your business."

"He sure didn't like me talking to you," Tyler said. "He looked like he wanted to punch me. Not your boyfriend, huh?"

I rolled my eyes. "He did not want to punch you."

"I caught that little move he did," Tyler said, grinning. "The way he put his hand on your neck it might as well have been a collar."

"You know what, Tyler?" I said, my face flushing. "Fuck off, okay?"

He only laughed. "Relax, Annie. I'm just messing around."

I glared at him.

"Look, I'll change the subject, okay? Word is, the suits are really excited about the press we're getting."

In spite of my irritation, I felt a little glow of excitement at that. We had been written up in the weekend section of the *Free Press* that morning. It had been a glowing review and I had been singled out. Jen cut it out and hung it on our refrigerator.

"If things keep going like this, we're a shoe-in for Chicago. The investors are meeting with Jenner next week."

"Do you think they'll re-cast?" I asked, deciding to forget how irritated I was with him.

Tyler shrugged. "Maybe some parts. I think you're safe, though. You seem to be coming out of this with bells on."

"What can I say," I said drily. "I'm destined to be a superstar."

"You joke, Annie, but I actually think that might be true."

Tyler motioned to the bartender to refill us.

"Seriously, you're really good. And you have the looks to go far, that's for sure." He looked me over in a way that normally would make me want to slap a guy, but something about the joking light in his eyes only made me laugh.

"Have you ever tried to get work in Chicago or New York?"

I shook my head. "I was never really interested, to tell you the truth. I like it here."

"Yeah, but how much opportunity is there to really act around here?"

"A lot," I said, feeling defensive about my city. "People are doing shows all over the place."

"Yeah, but none of them are going to make you famous."

"That's not really a consideration for me," I said.

Tyler burst out laughing. "Yeah, right," he said. "An actress who doesn't care about fame?"

"I'm serious," I told him.

"You might think that now, but just wait until we get to New York. You can't get off on standing up in front of a bunch of people, demanding their attention, if a part of you didn't like it. The need for validation is what drives all actors. It's in your blood."

I shrugged. "I don't know about that."

"You'll see," he said. "So, now that you're not mad at me anymore, can I ask about the suit?"

"Who?" I asked.

"The guy in the suit. Your not-boyfriend boyfriend. What's the story there?"

Now that I had another beer in me the thought of talking about Nate didn't bother me so much. "We met in Vegas," I told Tyler. "In September."

"But he's from here?"

"Yeah, Birmingham."

"What does he do?"

"He works for Ford. He's an engineer." Tyler smirked at that. "What? What's the matter with being an engineer?"

"Nothing," he said, holding up his hands. "Just doesn't quite seem your type. Suit-and-tie guy and all that."

"He's very nice to me," I said, feeling the need to defend Nate. But wasn't Tyler saying the same things I had thought from the beginning?

"So what happens when you go to New York?" he asked.

"What do you mean?"

"I mean, do you stay with this guy? Once you're in an off-Broadway run, living in the most exciting city in the world, how does that work out?"

"I don't know," I said, feeling uncomfortable. "I told you, we're just dating. It's not some serious thing."

"I hope not," Tyler said seriously. "I don't think you realize how much things will change when we hit it big, Annie. Guys like him, they just won't understand your life. Won't understand your art. You need someone more like you."

Without my noticing it, he had moved his hand over the bar until it was covering mine. There was a definite flirtatious light in his eyes as he looked at me.

I grabbed my hand back. "As a matter of fact," I said coldly. "I don't need anyone. Thanks for the advice though."

I grabbed my beer from the bar and made my way farther into the room, determined to be away for Tyler and his mocking, smug flirtation. He might be a cute guy, and he might be funny sometimes, but he was also kind of an asshole. And I didn't need that tonight.

"Hey, Annie," a voice said next to me.

I turned to find Jenner Collins smiling at me.

"Are you enjoying yourself?"

"Very much," I told him. He motioned for me to join him at his table. Over the past few weeks I had gotten over my intimidation in his presence—mostly.

"Did you see the write-up in the *Free Press* today?" he asked.

"Yeah. That was really cool," I said.

"You had a pretty nice mention. I was proud of you."

"Thank you," I said. "That's never happened to me before. I mean, some of our shows at Wayne had write-ups, but nothing like that."

"It's pretty cool," he agreed. "Especially the first couple of times. Eventually it starts to matter less, and you work on the things that mean something to you, you know? Rather than the things that bring you praise."

"Is that why you're in Detroit so much lately?" I asked.

He laughed. "Yeah, my agent is getting pretty annoyed with me, actually. He keeps sending me scripts, assuring me they'll all be the next big box office smash."

"Any catching your eye?" I asked. Selfishly I wondered how him taking a role would effect our show.

"Not really. I'll have to commit to something in the spring, or else I'll be running out of money to fund this kind of thing."

I laughed. "So, what projects are you interested in?" I asked.

I was surprised by how easy he was to talk to. Up close I noticed that his eyes were ever so slightly off-center. It made him less perfect, more human somehow.

"I actually have some really big plans," he said, leaning forward. "But I'd rather this didn't get out to everyone."

"Of course," I said, leaning forward myself. Maybe he was going to tell me that he wanted to shoot a movie here in Detroit, staring me. He would make me a rich movie star and I'd never even have to leave home.

"I want to start a permanent company in the city," he said. "With a home theater and resident artistic staff. We would put on original shows, try to bring in as many local writers as we could."

"That sounds amazing," I breathed. "Wow." It might not be as glamorous, but in all honesty, what he was describing was more appealing to me than the movie fantasy.

"I figured it'd be right up your alley," he said, nodding in approval. "You work at a local theater, don't you?"

I nodded. "The Springwells Theater Company. We mostly do education and outreach for local kids."

"I think having an education component would be important," he said. "We could run camps and classes, give back a little."

"Jenner, seriously, this sounds incredible," I said. I had never been good at selling myself or networking, but at that moment I didn't care. "If you need any help, please keep me in mind. I'd love to be involved in this."

Jenner smiled at me broadly. "I'm glad to hear that. You know, you're the first person in this cast who hasn't hinted to me about how willing you'd be to go to New York with the show."

I blushed a little. "I *would* be happy to go to New York," I said slowly. "I'd be happy to do anything that kept me acting. But a local company like this, with an outreach component...it sounds perfect."

"Well, I'll definitely keep you up to date with the details."

Over his shoulder I caught sight of Jasmine, glaring at me. I stifled a laugh, badly.

"What?" Jenner asked, looking over his shoulder.

"Nothing," I said. "I think someone is trying to crush my head with mind power."

Jenner must have caught sight of Jasmine because he turned back to me, rolling his eyes. "You'd think I'd be used to that garbage by now," he said. "Oh well, only a few more weeks, right?"

"Right," I said, happily thinking to myself that Jasmine might not be joining the cast in Chicago.

"I should really get going," he said, looking down at his watch. "I have a breakfast meeting pretty early."

"Thanks for the party, Jenner," I said sincerely. "And thanks for telling me about the company. Good luck with it."

Jenner clapped a hand on my shoulder. "Thank you for all of your hard work. It means a lot to me. See you tomorrow."

He turned and left, saying goodbye to people as he made his way through the crowds. I caught sight of

Jasmine struggling through the throng in an attempt to catch up with him.

For once I didn't feel at all grossed out by her. I was way too excited and happy to care much about anyone else. Jenner Collins thought I was doing a good job! And he wanted me to know about his company. What if he actually asked me to be a part of it?

I pictured myself, a year from now, teaching acting classes to kids. Without awful Grayson to boss me around, I could get out of the office and spend more time on the creative side. Maybe I'd even get the chance to perform, or at least work on some of the shows in some capacity. A group of resident artists. The very idea sent a shiver down my arms.

I compared my feelings with how I felt about the possibility of going to Chicago, or even New York. The idea of acting every night was definitely a dream come true. And this play was great. But if I could still act and got to stay here? I had to admit, if it came down to a choice between the two, it would be a very, very tough decision.

Chapter Twenty-two

'One of the best things you can do to solidify your new relationship is to create some new traditions with your man. The holidays are a great time to do this. Why not give him a taste of all the memories you're sure to create over the years once you have a family of your own? He may be hesitant at first—lots of guys think traditions aren't very masculine—but if you're persistent you can show him how much fun it can be!'—The Single Girl's Guide to Finding True Love

"Come on, Annie, I really think this will be fun."

"Nate, seriously? What the hell is fun about tramping around in the freezing cold to carry some sappy, half-dead tree home?"

"Why do you think it will be half-dead?" he asked, looking disappointed.

"Because it's almost Christmas. The trees in these lots are cheap rip-offs. Of course it will be half dead."

Nate shook his head at me. "You are way too cynical for your own good. Come on, Annie. Come pick out a Christmas tree with me."

I sighed. "Fine," I said. "But you have to stop and buy me hot chocolate on the way home."

He grinned. "Sold."

Minutes later, I was shivering while Nate walked up and down the rows of trees. A tree lot had sprung up a few weeks ago down the street from his apartment and he had been bugging me to go with him to find the perfect tree ever since.

"Hmm, we always get a nice blue spruce at home," he said, squinting at a tree in front of us. "What do you think this one is?"

"If you can't tell them apart, why do you care what kind you get?" I asked.

"It's tradition!" he replied, grabbing me around the waist to pull me close. "Come on, don't you have any traditions?"

I shrugged. "My mom had an ugly old silver fake tree that she would pull out every year and decorate while I was at school."

Nate looked at me with an expression akin to horror on his face. "Are you kidding me?" he asked.

"No," I said, pulling away. "Why would I be kidding?"

"You guys didn't put your tree up together? What about the eggnog? What about the cookies?"

"Nate, I was too old for that stuff by the time I was ten."

"No," he said seriously, shaking his head. "No, no, no. You're never too old for decorating a Christmas tree. Oh, Annie. Now my mission is clear to me. I must impress upon you the wonderfulness of Christmas traditions."

"Oh, Jesus," I muttered.

"Seriously, Annie. Some of my favorite memories are of putting up the tree. We would go out with my whole family, all my cousins and my aunts and uncles, and we'd find a good tree farm—"

"A what?"

"A tree farm," he said. "You know, a place you go to cut down trees."

"You actually went out in the woods with an axe to chop down your tree?" I asked him. "Are you sure you're not confusing your life with a Laura Ingalls book?"

He pulled on my earlobe, an annoying habit he had picked up to get back at me when I teased him.

"We did not go into the woods," he said with dignity. "We went to a tree farm."

"Like that's so much better," I muttered. He just looked at me. "Sorry," I said. "You were saying?"

"So we would all go out and find the perfect tree for each of our houses. And then we would take turns with the saw to cut them down. And after we got them all loaded up on top of the cars, we would go back to my aunt's house for pizza. It was so great."

"I guess you had to be there," I said drily. Nothing that he had described sounded remotely like fun to me.

"Maybe," he said. "Maybe next year we can go out to Maryland to visit them and you can come along for the tree-picking day."

I stared at him, aghast. He was not seriously making plans for us in a year—especially not for me to meet his entire family.

Before I could say anything, Nate started cracking up.

"Oh, you're too easy," he said. "God, it looked like your head was about to explode there, Annie."

"Haha," I replied, turning away. "You're such a laugh riot."

"Anyhow," he said as he grabbed my hand, undeterred. "The next weekend my dad would spend all day Saturday putting lights up on the tree. And he would complain the whole time because the needles were so prickly. Then he and my mom would fight about the tree—he would say that next year we were getting a scotch pine, something with softer bristles. And she would yell at him and say that the blue spruce was prettier and she would be damned if she would get anything else. And then he would say, 'Well you can put the lights up yourself then!'"

Nate's face suddenly turned wistful, the way it did when he would get carried away in telling a story about his dad. It was almost like he would forget for a few minutes why he was sad...

I squeezed his hand. "Would they make up?" I asked softly.

He shook his head almost imperceptibly, as if he was clearing it, then smiled down at me. "Yeah. By that night they would be snuggling in front of the lights. And then they'd have the exact same fight the next year."

"Who's doing the lights this year?" I asked, feeling suddenly guilty for monopolizing so much of his time when his mother probably wanted him at home.

"She got a fake tree," he said, his face clouding over a little. "The year after he died. One of those pre-lit ones. She can set it up all by herself."

Something about the story made me feel incredibly sad. I squeezed his hand again, determined to change the subject. "I'm freezing my butt off out here, Hughes," I said. "Let's pick that tree and get it home."

He smiled at me, a grateful smile, and started to lead me down the rows of trees. I squinted at the tags in the darkness, hoping I would find...

"Here," I said, tugging on his hand so he would stop. "This one looks perfect."

He looked at it for a long minute, his head cocked as if in serious consideration. "It does look pretty good."

"I think it's beautiful," I told him.

He peered down to look at the tag. "Blue spruce," he murmured.

"Your mom has good taste," I said.

Nate looked up at me, a grin spreading across his face. Then he leaned forward and kissed me.

"So do you," he said. "Come on, let's get this home."

***

We dragged the tree behind us on the sidewalk. My fingers were freezing around the trunk in spite of my warm mittens. "God, you owe me so big for this," I muttered. "I'm so cold!"

"Oh, stop being such a baby," he said, looking at me over his shoulder. "This is good for you. Fresh air, exercise..."

"Nate, it's five below," I said. "This isn't fresh air, it's torture."

"Such a baby," he said sadly.

We finally reached his apartment and dragged the tree up the stairs to the second floor. It wasn't until he was unlocking his door that I remembered what was missing. "Hey!" I said loudly. "You were supposed to get me a hot chocolate!"

"Not to fear," he said, opening the door and pulling the tree through. "I have hot chocolate right here in the house."

"Seriously?" I asked, following him in and stamping my boots on the welcome mat to rid them of their cover of snow. "What twenty-eight-year-old man keeps cocoa in his house?"

"I've got marshmallows, too," he said happily. He raised one eyebrow at me in a mock-seductive expression. "You know you think that's sexy."

I couldn't help but laugh. "Oh yeah, baby," I replied.

Nate pulled the tree into the living room.

"Don't you need one of those stand things?" I asked him.

"Yes," he replied. "And I have one."

"Where?" I asked, surprised.

"In my Christmas decoration box," he said.

"Oh my God," I said, collapsing on the couch. "You have a decoration box? Who are you?"

"Let me rephrase that," Nate said. "I have several decoration boxes."

When I stared at him incredulously, he only smiled. "Annie, trust me," he said. "Christmas is the best time of year. This is going to be fun."

I shrugged my shoulders. "If you say so..."

Twenty minutes later, Nate had pulled several plastic tubs up from his storage cage in the basement and set the tree up in a red metal stand. Now he was pulling out string after string of lights.

"I have a feeling your dad had a point," I said, gingerly touching one of the branches. "These needles are sharp as hell."

"It builds character," he said bracingly.

But a few minutes later he was asking me for my mittens in an effort to protect his hands.

"These don't help," he said grumpily. "The needles just poke right through."

"Do you have any hockey gloves?" I asked.

"No," he muttered, wincing again as he struggled to wrap the wire around one of the top branches. "Crap, that hurts!"

"I have an idea," I said, pulling the lights from his hand. "Instead of wrapping, let's go for a more artistic drape." I started to lay the strand on top of the braches, pulling it around the tree as I went.

"Smart girl," Nate said, taking the lights back and continuing to drape the strand. When he was finished I plugged the lights in and we both stood back to admire it.

"Well," Nate said. "Maybe not quite as nice as my dad did it, but still not bad."

"Okay," I said, looking around at the boxes. "What now?"

"Now," Nate said excitedly. "We put some music on and we start to decorate!"

Before I could respond, Nate had hurried off to the bedroom. A few minutes later he came back with his iPod, which he plugged into the docking stereo. The strains of Nat King Cole's 'Christmas Song' soon filled the room.

"I'm not even going to say it," I said, staring at him.

"What, you think it's lame I have Christmas music on my iPod?"

I just shook my head at him. "Hide your true feelings all you want," he said, bending down to rifle through one of the boxes. "But I know you think I'm adorable."

I would never admit it, but the truth was, I kind of did.

"Get over here," he said, putting his hands on his hips and looking at me sternly. "You're helping, missy."

I groaned, but got up and joined him. "Is there, like, some specific traditional order we need to follow here?" I asked.

"Nope," he said. "Just grab one and get going."

Nate had a lot of ornaments. And most of them had a story, which he insisted on sharing with me. "I got that one in Frankenmuth," he told me, pointing at the glass bulb in my hand. "The year after I moved here. My sister Emily came out to visit and we went to that Christmas store, you know, the one that's open all year?"

I nodded. Frankenmuth was a touristy little town about two hours away. They got *really* into Christmas up there.

"We took Danny to see Santa there last year," I told him.

Nate laughed. "My mom still writes 'from Santa' on half of our gifts."

I snorted. "When I was seven I told my mom to give up the act."

He stared at me, aghast. "You were only seven?"

I shrugged, feeling uncomfortable. That was the year I asked Santa to make my dad leave his newest girlfriend. When he didn't come home for Christmas, I decided I'd had enough of the fat man in the red suit.

Nate must have noticed I was uncomfortable—he had gotten surprisingly adept at that—and he changed the subject.

"So, that ornament," he said, pointing to the misshapen clay lump in my hand, "was a gift from my sister Janna. She made it when she was six."

"What is it?" I asked, holding it up to the light.

"I think it was supposed to be a reindeer," he said, squinting at it.

I felt a rush of affection for him, this man that would keep such a gift for all these years, a man who would cart it all the way from Maryland to Michigan and put it on his tree. I watched him as he hung a red glitter bulb on a tall branch. The lights from the tree reflected in his blond hair.

"Nate," I said suddenly.

He looked at me, smiling slightly. "Yeah?"

I kissed him, holding onto his face for a long moment as I pressed my lips against his.

"What was that for?" he asked, when I finally pulled away. He had a slightly dazed look on his face, but he was smiling at me.

"Nothing," I said, grinning back. "I just felt like kissing you."

It took us about twenty minutes to finish the tree. Sometimes we talked, Nate telling me about ornaments or memories they invoked. Mostly we worked in comfortable silence, the soft strains of Christmas music the only sound in the room.

When we were done, Nate went to the kitchen to make us some cocoa. He joined me on the couch a few minutes later with a mug for each of us, and a plate of cookies. "Those look homemade," I told him, already imagining him in a frilly apron whipping up a batch of cookies.

"You can stop that right now," he said, as if reading my mind. "My mom sent these this morning."

He turned all the lamps off in the apartment so the only light was coming from the tree. You could barely tell we had phoned it in with the strings of lights; with the ornaments on, the tree looked perfect.

"Come here," Nate said, pulling me against him on the couch. I snuggled against his chest, subconsciously finding the now familiar place where I fit perfectly.

"Thank you for doing this with me," he whispered, kissing the top of my head.

"Thank you for making me," I told him.

"You had fun, didn't you?" he asked. I couldn't see his face, but I could tell that he was smiling.

"Yeah," I whispered. "I had a lot of fun."

We stayed like that for a long time, sitting in front of the tree with the music playing softly, Nate's arms around me. I snuggled closer to him, feeling happy. Feeling so happy that it scared me.

Chapter Twenty-three

*'Are you the type of girl who always puts her girlfriends first? While those relationships should be precious to you, it is essential that you learn to put your man first. No self-respecting gentleman wants to play second fiddle to your female friends!'—**The Single Girl's Guide to Finding True Love***

"Nate, it's Annie," I said after Nate's voicemail had picked up. "Listen, I know we had talked about hanging out tonight, but I have to cancel. Jen and Ginny both have the morning off tomorrow, which never happens. So we're going out tonight. Sorry, babe. I'll make it up to you, okay? Call me."

I hung up, feeling a slight twinge of regret. Since the show had started its run, I was pretty tied up most weekends. With Nate working late most weeknights, we weren't seeing each as much as we would have liked.

But I hadn't seen the girls in even longer, so it was really no contest.

Ginny came over to get ready with us, and it was almost like old times. Tina had already moved out, and it was feeling more like our house again. I was determined to enjoy it until Matt moved in.

I had agreed to Jen's plan, feeling like I didn't really have much choice. It didn't seem ideal for me, but what could I do? Tell Jen no, we needed to find another roommate? What if she decided she wanted to live with Matt more than me? What would I do then?

Besides, if the show did end up going to Chicago, I wouldn't be around for awhile. And I couldn't leave Jen in the lurch like that. So Matt had begun the process of buying the house from our landlord, who was happy enough to get it off his hands in this market. They were closing in two weeks.

I tried to push all of that out of my mind, though. Tonight was girls' night, and I was really excited.

"What do you think about this?" Ginny asked, coming out of the bathroom in a flowing, frumpy prairie dress.

"Where the hell did you get that thing?" I asked her.

"It was in your closet," she responded.

I squinted at it, and in fact did remember buying it last summer. But I usually wore it with a scarf belted around the waist, to make it look less...voluminous. And I certainly never wore it with a cardigan, the way Ginny was now.

"It's not really you, Gin," I told her, struggling to be polite and wishing Jen would hurry up and get out here. She was much better at this type of thing. I was more likely to tell Ginny that she looked ridiculous.

"I just feel like all of my clothes are too immature," she said, sighing. "I still dress like I'm in college. I mean, I'm a mom now. Shouldn't I be dressing like it?"

"Okay, who the hell are you and what did you do with my best friend?" I asked, unable to play polite anymore. Ginny was the most fashion-conscious girl I knew. Her favorite pastime in the world was to troll through sample sales and resale stores to get her hands on designer stuff that fit her budget. She didn't dress slutty, but she did like to show off her figure—and I couldn't blame her there.

"Josh's mom said something to me," she said, walking into my room and flopping down on the bed."

"Mrs. Stanley?" I asked, feeling angry at the very mention of her name. That woman had very nearly ruined Ginny's life, not to mention Danny's.

"She was over yesterday; they'd been on vacation and she wanted to drop off some presents for Josh and Danny. Anyhow, she gave me this frumpy old sweatshirt from Miami Beach. I mean, who goes to Miami and comes back with a sweatshirt?"

"Evil old hags," I said, eager for her to get to the juicy part.

"Yeah, you're telling me. So basically after she gives it to me she looks me over, totally judgmental, and says something about how she thought of me when she saw it because she figured I'd be grateful for something more appropriate."

"God, what a bitch," I said. "Where was Josh when this was going on?"

"Outside with his dad, looking at his car. He's been having carburetor trouble."

"Did you tell him what she said?"

Ginny just shrugged. "He would only get mad. Their relationship is bad enough as it is."

Josh, to his credit, had not forgiven his parents for their meddling. They rarely saw them, and I knew Ginny felt guilty about this.

"Virgina McKensie, it is not your fault that his mother is a horrible witch," I said firmly. "Don't you go feeling guilty for what she did. And for God's sake, don't listen to a word she says. She's just jealous that she's a dried-up old hag while you're still hot, even after having a baby. So screw her, okay?"

"You're right," Ginny said, giving me a watery little smile. "I just don't want to embarrass Danny when he gets bigger. I don't want to be one of those middle-aged women who still think they're teenagers."

"When you start wearing tube tops to the playground I promise I'll put a stop to it, okay?"

"Deal," she said.

"Now please, take that dress off and throw it away. I can never look at it the same way again."

In the end, Ginny picked a black tank top dotted with sequins. She paired it with a pair of tight boot-cut jeans and tall black heels. Needless to say, she was a total knockout—and not the least bit inappropriate.

"You look great," she said, looking me over.

My tastes were a bit more eclectic than my friends, and I had settled on a vintage sixties-style dress that I had ordered online. It was very mod and I loved it.

"I feel dressed down next to the two of you," Jen said once she'd joined us, looking down at her black pants and white button-up top.

"Add some jewelry," Ginny advised, apparently over her fashion crisis and ready to be our guru again. "That will dress it up. And for God's sake, unbutton a few of those buttons."

We ended up at a Mexican restaurant that we all liked. They served huge margaritas (the basis of their appeal) and kept free refills coming on their homemade tortillas and salsa.

"So, only two more weeks of the run," Jen said after she had sampled her margarita. "Are you sad or relieved?"

"I guess that depends on what happens next," I said.

"Still no word on Chicago?"

"Only rumors," I said. "Nothing will happen until after Christmas, so I'm trying not to think about it too much."

"What does Nate think?" Ginny asked casually.

"We haven't really talked about," I said, shrugging.

"Don't you think you should?" she pressed.

"Why?"

"Well, don't you want to know where you stand?"

"Ginny," I said, sighing. "Why do we have to keep having this conversation? I know where I stand. We have fun together and we like to spend time together. Nothing more, nothing less. Why is that so hard for you to understand?"

"Because I know you," she said, her voice suddenly firm. "Better than just about anyone. So I can tell when you're spouting bullshit."

I stared at her. Where had that come from?

"I would rather not talk about this anymore," I said flatly.

"Too bad," she said. "Because I want to."

"Okay, girls," Jen said wearily. She'd had many years of experience diffusing mine and Ginny's bickering. We were best friends and we loved each other to death, but we'd also known each other since we were five. A bit of bickering was only to be expected, I guess. "Let's order first, and then we can choose a topic, okay?"

I looked down at my menu, feeling irritated with Ginny for reasons I couldn't really put into words. I knew that she loved me and had my best interests at heart, but it really bugged me when she acted like she knew what I was feeling better than I did.

After our waitress took our order, Ginny leaned back in her chair. "Look," she said. "I didn't mean to piss you off. I just don't understand why you feel like you can't be honest about this kind of stuff with us."

"Are you calling me a liar now?" I asked, color flooding my cheeks.

She just rolled her eyes at me. "Stop being a drama queen," she scoffed. "All I'm saying is you seem to be terrified to tell us that you have feelings for someone, even when we all can see that you do. What do you think, that we're going to judge you or something?"

"I don't think you'll judge me," I said.

"Do you think it will mess up your tough girl reputation?" she pressed.

"Jesus, Ginny," I muttered, not liking this conversation one bit.

"Nate is crazy about you," she said. "Anyone can see it. He's totally fallen for you. And I can see you starting to sweat right now, just from me bringing it up. So I think that's something we should deal with."

"I just..." I stammered, not knowing how to respond. "It freaks me out, okay?" I finally snapped.

"Okay," she said, smiling at me.

"Something funny about that?"

"No, I'm just happy that you told me something real."

I glared at her and didn't respond.

"Listen to me, okay? You don't have to respond and you can hate me when I'm done, but you need to hear this." She waited until I met her gaze before she continued. "I get that all the stuff that went down with your dad made you feel freaked out about guys—"

"Oh, God," I said, throwing my napkin down. "Can we please not have the whole 'her-dad-abandoned-her-so-she-mistrusts-men' conversation? It's so cliché. And not true."

"I was actually talking more about your mom," she said sharply.

That shut me up.

"I know that you're terrified of being like her. We both do." She gestured to Jen, who looked at me sadly. "We understand that, okay?"

"No you don't," I said quietly. "You didn't live with her after he left. You don't know what that was like."

"No, but my parents did have their own special set of issues," she said flatly. "And so did Jen's."

I fell silent at that. Ginny was totally right, of course. She had a terrible relationship with her parents, had since she was a little kid. They never approved of anything she did, and in response, she acted out like crazy. Partying, drinking, hooking up with random guys—that was Ginny's life until she met Josh.

Jen, on the other hand, had parents who were crazy about her. But her father's alcohol addiction had destroyed their family and nearly killed him. Her mom had turned into a work-obsessed robot in order to cope, and did her best to pass those traits off onto Jen.

"Did you ever think that there's a reason the three of us are friends?" Jen asked quietly.

"We're friends because Ginny and I lived on the same street since we were babies," I said, not interested in some pseudo-psych babble. "Then we met you in high school and the three of us hit it off."

"That's why we *became* friends," Jen said, refusing to be put off by my tone. "But why are we *still* friends? How many of the girls we went to high school with are still close with their former best friends? Who do you know that stayed as close as we are?"

"No one," Ginny agreed.

"We stayed this close because we became each other's families," Jen continued. "We all came from screwed-up homes, right? None of us had someone in our family to connect with. We all *needed* someone when we met."

I had a sudden mental image of Ginny sneaking into my house when we were ten. I had finally admitted to her that I was having nightmares when my dad was gone. So for two months one summer she snuck into my room every night after her parents had tucked her in and slept in my bed with me. I met her eyes, and I knew she was thinking about the same thing.

"All I'm saying," she said softly, "is that we know you, Annie. You're our family. So you can talk to us about stuff." She paused. "And you don't have to get mad at me when I tell you this: if you keep throwing away guys the way you've always done, you're going to end up every bit as unhappy as she is."

I stared at her, taking in her words as my heart sank. Everything I had done since I was thirteen years old had been an effort to escape my mother's fate. And now Ginny was telling me that it was hopeless, that I was going to end up like her anyhow. The thought made me sick.

"Don't throw Nate away," she said softly. "That's the last thing I'm going to say on the subject. But please think about it, okay?"

I nodded, unable to speak. Luckily, the waiter arrived with our food and I was spared the rest of the conversation. Jen deftly steered discussion away to safer matters—something ridiculous that Kiki had done in front of a client. As Jen talked, Ginny laughed and drank her margarita like nothing had happened.

But under the table, she reached out and grabbed my hand. And she didn't let go for a very long time.

Chapter Twenty-four

"Annie, can you come in and talk with me for a minute?"

I looked up to see Jenner Collins standing in the doorway to my dressing room.

"Sure," I told him. "I'm just about done here."

I swept the rest of my cosmetics back into their case and stood up from the dressing table. We had just wrapped the second-to-last Sunday matinee of the run. Next weekend we were closing. So far I hadn't heard anything but rumors regarding the fate of our show after this run, but looking up at Jenner I had a feeling that was about to change.

Jenner gestured for me to follow him, and headed down the hall to the small room he had been using as an office. Tabitha was sitting there on one side of his makeshift desk, and he gestured for me to join her, going around to sit across from us.

"I'm sure you've heard all the rumors about Chicago," he said, not wasting any time.

I nodded. "People are saying the announcement is imminent," I told him.

"Well, the gossipers are bound to get it right once in a while," Tabitha said drily. I looked at her in surprise. Did that mean...

"Annie, we're taking the show to Chicago in the New Year to do an eight week run," Jenner said. "Beyond that, we have investors showing a lot of interest in New York. If the Chicago run goes well, we could be off-Broadway by the spring."

"Wow," I said. "Congratulations, Jenner. That's a huge accomplishment."

He smiled at me from across the desk. "Annie, we think you've done a wonderful job in this show. We really couldn't be more pleased. We'd be very happy if you came to Chicago with us to reprise the role."

I stared at him for a minute, trying to form words.

Tabitha laughed next to me, the most human thing I had ever heard her do. "I think you've shocked her," she said, smiling at me.

"Oh my God," I finally whispered. "This is for real?"

"It is," Jenner said. "We'll all be off for the holidays then get started in Chicago the first week of the New Year. I hope you'll be with us."

"Of course I will," I said quickly. "Of course. Thank you so much. This is amazing. Thank you."

"You're quite welcome," Jenner said, standing up and holding out his hand to shake mine. Tabitha followed his lead and did the same. "We'll see you next Friday for the closing weekend. Enjoy this, Annie, but remember that we still have work to do."

"Of course," I said. "I won't forget that."

I left the office, feeling like my feet weren't touching the ground. This was amazing. I was going to Chicago!

I didn't stick around the theater long enough to see if anyone else had been offered a spot. I had to get home to talk to the girls.

***

I made the drive from the city to our house in record time. I was relieved to see Jen's car in the driveway. I thought of calling Ginny and asking her to meet us, but she generally worked at the bookstore on Sunday. I would have to wait.

"Jen?" I called as I opened the front door.

"Up here!" she called from the second floor. I ran up the stairs as quickly as I could.

"Oh my God, Jen, you'll never—"

I stopped in the doorway to the upstairs bedroom. Jen and Matt were sitting on the carpet, pieces of metal spread out in front of them. They appeared to be building something. "What're you doing?" I asked.

"Matt bought a new bed at Ikea," Jen said. She didn't look quite like herself, and it took a minute for me to realize that she was actually disheveled. She had her hair up under a bandana, and was wearing paint-splattered clothes. I could count on one hand the number of times I had seen Jen Campbell look anything but perfectly put-together, and the sight threw me.

"Then he lost the directions," Jen continued, laughing. He grinned at her sheepishly. "So yeah, we're trying to figure out how to put this thing together."

My brain, on complete overdrive from Jenner's news, took a moment to process what she was saying. In all of my excitement I had completely forgotten what was happening at the house today—Matt was moving in. Looking around the room, I saw boxes stacked against the walls. Jen and Matt were going to live up here, in Ginny's old room, which was much larger than Jen's current room downstairs.

"Oh," I said, feeling off-balance. "Of course."

But Matt and Jen were barely listening to me. Their attention had returned to the project in front of them. "Seriously, Matt?" Jen said, laughing. "You really think you should just start hammering when these two pieces clearly don't fit together?"

"I don't see you with any better solution," he said. But he didn't sound annoyed. They both looked totally pleased with themselves, with each other. Normally Jen would be going nuts over anything this disorganized. Instead, I had the feeling she was having the time of her life, here with Matt trying to build a bed in their new room together.

Something about the way they looked at each other, the happiness that exuded from the pair of them, made my heart clench. They were moving in together. Taking the next step. They were in love and they were starting a life together.

I want that.

The realization, which seemed to come from nowhere, hit me like a punch to the gut. I literally took a step backwards in surprise.

"Annie, what's wrong?" Jen asked, finally noticing that one person in the room wasn't involved in their little love-fest.

"Nothing, sorry," I said, barely hearing my own voice over the rushing that had started in my ears. "A little dizzy."

"Sit down," Jen demanded, moving to stand up.

"No, I'm just gonna go down to my room," I said quickly. "I'm fine."

Before she could respond, I was fleeing back down the stairs, suddenly feeling like I might throw up.

What had just happened? How could one moment suddenly change the way I saw everything in my life? If there was anything I had ever been sure of, it was this: love is a waste of time and energy. While it might make a select few happy (a very select few), it was most definitely not for me. Never had been, never would be.

I sat down on the edge of my bed, trying to gather my thoughts, to make sense of what I had just experienced, but my brain felt jumbled. One thing was clear to me: in that moment of watching Jen and Matt, I finally figured it out. I wanted what they had—I wanted it with Nate.

I wanted it so bad the thought of going to Chicago made me feel panicky.

"What the hell am I doing?" I whispered. "What's wrong with me?"

"Annie?" Jen's voice called from outside my door. "Can I come in?"

"Sure," I said, surprised at how calm my voice sounded.

She opened my door and peered into the room. "Are you okay?"

"Yeah," I said, managing a smile. "I didn't eat much before the show this morning. I think it finally hit me. But I'm fine."

I wasn't quite sure why I was lying to her. All I knew was that I didn't want to have this conversation with Matt in the house.

"Let me make you something to eat," she said, still sounding worried. "You look really pale."

"I'll grab a sandwich," I told her. "Don't worry."

"Okay," she said, looking uncertain. "If you're sure."

"Jen, you ready?" Matt called from the living room.

"We need to run to the hardware store," she told me. "In addition to the directions, we also appear to be missing several essential screws." She laughed, but stopped when she saw my face. "You really do look pale. How about I send Matt and stay here with you?"

"I'm fine," I told her. "Seriously. God knows he'll come home with the wrong stuff if you aren't there to supervise."

She smiled. "That's probably true. Are you sure you're—"

"I'm fine. Go."

She smiled at me one more time before closing the door. A moment later, I heard soft giggling from the living room, then the sound of the front door shutting.

The sound made me feel very lonely somehow, and I instantly regretted sending her away. I should have just asked her if Matt could take off for a while so we could talk. I needed her to talk me down, help me figure out what was happening in my head. I felt like the world had readjusted itself around me, leaving me off-balance and terrified.

Ginny, I thought. I needed to call Ginny.

No sooner had I picked up the phone than it began ringing. I looked down at the display, my thoughts immediately going to Nate.

It was my mother.

Suddenly I was desperate to talk to her, desperate to tell her how scared I was. For the first time since I had been a very small child, I felt a yearning for my mother, for her to tell me that everything would be okay.

"Hi, Mom," I said into the phone, trying to regulate the rapid beating of my heart.

"Hi, honey!" she said, excitement clear in her voice. "How are you?"

"I'm pretty good," I said, taking a deep breath. "I'm really glad you called. I wanted to—"

"Oh, sweetie, I just have the best news," she interrupted, not really listening. "You'll never believe who I had lunch with today!"

I groaned inwardly. It figured. Just when I actually needed her, she was going to go on and on about some old biddy from her sewing group. "Who, Mom?" I asked, figuring I might as well let her get her story over with.

"Your father!"

If I thought my revelation upstairs had thrown me for a loop, it was nothing compared to this. My heart, which a moment ago had been beating alarmingly fast, now seemed to stop altogether.

"What?" I whispered.

"Your daddy! He called me up yesterday, can you believe it? And asked me if I wanted to have lunch today. So of course, I said yes. I mean, like I would refuse!" She laughed a little, a twinkly girlish laugh that made me feel nauseous. "It was so sweet, honey, he picked me up and took me that restaurant we all used to like, you know—"

"Mom!" I exclaimed, unable to take it anymore. Was she seriously telling me this?

"What?" my mother asked, bewildered.

"I don't care where he took you," I said, struggling to keep my voice even. My hands were shaking so hard I thought I might drop my phone. "I don't care how sweet he was or what he said. He's an adulterous bastard who abandoned us, remember?"

"Annie Duncan, I don't want to hear that kind of talk," she said, her voice hardening. "He may have made mistakes, but I'm sure he's sorry."

"I don't care if he's sorry," I spat. "I don't want to hear *anything* about him."

"I don't know what's gotten into you," she said. "I thought you'd be pleased. It's been so long since you've seen him."

"Because he left us!" I bellowed. "God, what the hell is wrong with you?"

"I will not be spoken to like that," she said, her voice tight. "I am your mother."

"I can't have this conversation with you," I said. My anger at her, at my father, was so great it actually scared me. "I'll talk to you later."

Before she could respond, I hung up. I stared down at the phone for a minute, trying to wrap my mind around what she had just said. My mother had seen my dad. She had let him—what, take her out on a date? I felt rage boiling up in me until I couldn't take it anymore.

"Damn it!" I yelled, throwing my phone at the wall.

I heard the clatter as the case fell off and the battery came loose. I had probably ruined it. I couldn't care less.

I buried my head in my hands, trying to quell the overwhelming anger and fear that was coursing through me.

"Annie?"

I looked up and saw Nate standing there in my doorway, concern written all over his face.

"What's the matter?"

He looked so solid, standing there in my doorway. All I wanted in that moment was to go to him. To wrap my arms around him and tell him everything. To let him comfort me and promise me that he would stay with me, that he wouldn't leave.

But I couldn't.

"What are you doing here?" I whispered.

"I thought we were going shopping," he said, taking a step into the room. I had a vague recollection of making those plans this morning, before I left his apartment. "What's the matter?"

"I just..." I breathed heavily, trying to get myself under control. Between what had happened in Jen's room and my reaction to my mom, I knew I was acting like a crazy person.

"Sorry," I told him. "I just had a fight with my mom. No big deal."

"Are you sure?" he asked, coming to sit next to me.

The urge to throw myself into his arms was so overwhelming I had to stand to get away from him. He looked at me in confusion.

"Annie?"

"It's been a crazy day," I said, going over to stand next to my dresser, as far from him as I could get.

"Did the matinee go okay?"

"Yeah, it was fine," I said. "When it was over they..." I looked over at him, his face expectant and more than a little concerned. It would be so easy. So easy to forget about my mom, to tell him how I felt. To beg him to wait for me while I was in Chicago, or better yet, not go at all.

Not go at all.

That one errant thought had the effect, finally, of pulling me out of this craziness. Was I seriously considering not going to Chicago because of a guy? Giving up my dream so I could stay home and be in love? For some girls, it would be a no brainer. Romantic, silly girls. Girls who weren't like me.

It's what my mother would do. She would sacrifice anything for the man she loved, even her own happiness. Even the happiness of her child.

But I sure as hell wouldn't.

"Annie, will you please tell me what's going on?" he said, sounding almost scared.

"I'm moving to Chicago," I said. "And after that, hopefully New York. The play is moving on and I'm going with it."

I tried not to notice how excited he looked, how pleased he seemed to be for me. There was still worry in his face, sure, but the predominant emotion was clearly happiness. Like he wanted only what was good for me.

"Listen," I said, holding up my hand as he appeared about to get up. I was pleased to hear how steady my voice sounded. I was doing the right thing.

"I've been thinking about this a lot. I really don't want to do the whole long distance thing. It's not my style."

His expression clouded over and I turned my head slightly so I wouldn't have to see his face.

"I had a good time with you, Nate, I really did. But I think this has run its course."

He was silent for so long I finally had to chance a glance in his direction. He was staring at me, steely-eyed.

"What happened today?" he asked, his voice low.

"What do you mean?" I stammered.

"You weren't in this place when you left my bed this morning," he said.

I had a sudden memory of him handing me a coffee and kissing me at his door when I left for the theater, his hair tousled and his face rough with stubble. Was that only this morning? I pushed the image from my mind.

"When they offered me the chance to go to Chicago, it really clarified things for me," I said, careful to keep my voice emotionless. "It would be wrong of me to string you along when my focus is going to be elsewhere."

"Chicago is an hour's flight away," he said. "And the show won't run forever."

"Yeah, but when it's over we might be going to New York. Besides, you work during the week and I'll be performing on the weekends. It just won't work."

"It could," he said, his voice low. "If we worked at it—"

"I don't want to work at it!" I said, feeling my control slip a notch. "I want to work at doing the best show I can. That's all I can care about right now, okay?"

"I don't understand why you're doing this," he said, and something in his voice made me look at him again. I wished I hadn't. "I don't understand why you feel like you need to throw us away."

"What are you talking about?" I asked, starting to get pissed. "Nate, we were never serious. At least, I never was. I thought we wanted the same thing: some fun."

Suddenly he was on his feet and striding toward me. "Bullshit," he said, grabbing my arm so tight I yelped.

"Hey!" I cried, but he interrupted me.

"That's bullshit and you know it, Annie. Jesus, for such an amazing actor you'd think this song and dance would be a bit more believable."

"What are you talking about?" I demanded.

He released my arm and turned away from me. "You care about me. I know you do. You can pretend you don't all you want, but I know it's true. So what the hell is this all about, really?"

"You don't know what you're talking about," I said, shaking my head.

"I think I do," he said, his voice so angry I felt almost scared. "I think I know exactly what's going on. You're falling for me. The same way I'm falling for you. You know that we could be really amazing together and that scares the shit out of you."

"Why would that scare me?" I asked, my hands starting to shake.

He turned back to me and met my gaze evenly. "Because you think I'm going to leave you. And so you're determined to push me away first."

I stared back at him. "That's...that just ridiculous."

He laughed humorlessly. "Please. Don't insult me. It's fine, okay, if you think that. You could have the decency to just tell me. But don't pretend like I'm nothing, like we're nothing. Because we're not. And you know it. You fucking *know* it, Annie."

I felt like the wind had been knocked out of me. I had ditched tons of boys before and no one had ever said these things to me. No one had ever stood up and actually fought to keep me around.

Your mom fought, a little voice in my head said. *Look how hard she fought for dad. How long she fought. And where the hell did that get her? Alone and miserable and still pining after him, eager to accept his crumbs. After everything he did. Is that what you want?*

"No," I whispered. "I won't do this."

"Annie—"

"Nate, I'm sorry, but it's over. I don't want to be tied to home right now. I'm going to Chicago and that's the end."

"You know what, Annie?" Nate said, taking another step closer. He was only inches away now, so close I could see the wetness gathering in his eyes.

"You're a scared little girl. I never would have thought it of you, but you're nothing more than a coward."

I would have rather he slapped me, so great was the sting of his words. Before I could respond, he had turned away, was striding to the open bedroom door.

"Good luck with the show," he said, the bitterness in his voice palpable. Then he slammed the door to my room behind him and I was alone.

Chapter Twenty-five

*'The time after a break-up can be incredibly difficult. If you think you've finally found the one and it ends up not working out, it's easy to get discouraged. Don't become bitter, ladies! My advice to you is to get right back out there and start dating again!'—**The Single Girl's Guide to Finding True Love***

"Refill?" the waitress asked, holding up her coffee pot.

"Yes, please," I said, smiling at her.

She refilled my cup and ambled back to the counter. It was dead slow in the diner and I saw her pull out a magazine before she slipped behind the counter.

I turned back to my computer, trying to focus on the email from my mother. My moving to Chicago was what finally got her to brave her fear of the internet and get an email account. I was afraid I had unleashed a monster; she was now constantly sending me links to recipes she thought I should try (completely ignoring the fact that I couldn't cook) and articles detailing the wonder of internet dating.

Her first few emails had been chock-full of information about my father, but I told her flat-out I would delete anything else she sent me about him. Apparently, they were spending quite a bit of time together. How romantic.

My phone rang, distracting me from that line of thinking before I could get too angry. I looked down at the screen and smiled, though I also felt a little pang in my chest. Ginny.

"Hey, hon," I said.

"Annie Duncan, you little tart," she greeted me.

"Well, it's nice to hear from you too, Gin," I said.

"Do you know what I'm looking at right now?" she asked.

"Uh, no?"

"I'm looking at TMZ online. And what do you think I see on TMZ online?"

"God, Ginny, I have no idea. Is it something about sparkly vampires?"

"No, it's something about a Hollywood movie star seen out and about with an unknown woman. Do you know anything about this?"

I groaned. "Oh, geez."

"Seriously, how could you not have told me?" Ginny demanded.

"Told you what?"

"That you're dating Jenner Collins!"

"Ginny, I am not dating Jenner Collins. Give me a break."

"Well, according to TMZ, several inside sources have reported that you're his new love interest. This picture of the two of you was taken leaving a club at one o'clock in the morning Friday night. And sources said you were all over each other inside."

Okay, that made me freeze in my seat. "Are you kidding me?" I asked. "It says that?"

"Yes!" Ginny replied. "God, I can't believe it. My best friend, dating a movie star. Do you think you guys will invite Edward Pattinson to the wedding? Will you introduce me?"

"Ginny," I said firmly. "I am not dating Jenner Collins. There were about a dozen of us at that club that night. And there was certainly no being all over each other. I barely saw him inside."

"Really?" she asked, sounding disappointed.

"Really," I said.

"Man, I was hoping it was true. I would love to meet some celebrities."

"Sorry to disappoint you."

"Oh, that's okay," she said, sighing. "Anyways, how's it going over there?"

"It's pretty good," I told her. "We're still getting good reviews. Jenner says the suit guys are happy. It's looking like New York is more and more of a possibility."

"That's awesome," Ginny said. "I mean, it sucks for me. I already miss you like crazy and you're only a few hours away. What will I do when you're all the way on the East Coast?"

"You're telling me," I said, taking a sip of my coffee. "At least you have Jen and Josh. And Danny." I felt a sharp pain when I said his name. It had been nearly two months now, and I missed that kid so much it hurt. "I'm by myself."

She paused, and I had a horrible feeling she was going to bring up Nate. Instead she said, "You're not hitting it off with anyone else in the cast?"

"We get along okay," I said. "But none of them are best friend material."

Most of the cast had carried over from Detroit, including Tyler, but I spent very little time with any of them outside of the theater. What was the point?

"I'm sorry, hon," she said. "We really miss you."

"I miss you, too," I told her, afraid I was going to start crying.

Suddenly I heard a loud crash from Ginny's end of the phone.

"Damn," she muttered. "Danny, don't you dare touch that!"

"What happened?"

"He knocked over the coffee table," she sighed. "Which just so happened to have my coffee *on* it. I should go before he gets into the mess."

"Okay," I told her, wishing I was there with her. "Give him a hug for me, okay?"

"I will," she said. "Next time we talk I'll put him on the phone. He's saying so many words lately. Danny!" she called again. "Mommy said no!"

"Go," I told her. "Talk to you soon."

As soon as we were off the phone, I navigated away from my email. I had to see the pictures that Ginny had mentioned. I opened the entertainment site and sure enough, there I was. The picture had definitely been taken Friday night as we left the club. Jenner had his arm out, holding the door for me. From the angle they had taken it, it looked like he had his arm around me. I had a fleeting thought of Nate seeing this. I wondered what he would think.

"So there's the new love interest of Jenner Collins."

I looked up and saw Tyler standing in front of my table. "Hey," I told him.

"I'm assuming you've seen it?' he asked, grabbing a chair and sitting down.

"I'm looking at it now," I said, shaking my head. "These people are ridiculous."

"I'd be happy if I were you," he said. "I mean, this could be really good for you career-wise."

"How is getting my picture snapped with Jenner good for my career?"

"It's getting your name out there!" he said.

I pointed at the screen. "They're calling me an unknown twenty-year-old."

"So call them and tell them your name," he said. "Or have your agent do it. I guarantee this won't be the end of it."

"You're ridiculous," I told him. "I don't want to be tabloid fodder, thank you."

"Ah, I forgot. Annie is so above the seedier side of our business."

"What are you doing here, Tyler?" I asked, feeling tired of the conversation already.

"I knew you'd be here," he said, leaning forward on his elbows. "You hang out in this little dump every day, don't you?"

"My apartment is freezing," I told him. Which was true, but only part of the reason I frequented this diner. The free Wi-Fi was a perk, but in truth, it was just really nice to be around people. My apartment was empty and lonely.

"Well, tomorrow night I think you should get out of that freezing apartment and come hang out with me," he said.

I stared at him. "Are you asking me out?"

"Oh, come on, Annie," he said, rolling his eyes. "I've been asking you out since the first rehearsal. I know you left things badly with suit-and-tie guy, so I've been trying to give you your space. But we've been here two months now. Let's have some fun."

His casual mention of Nate sent my stomach plummeting. It had been like that ever since I got here. Something would happen to remind me of him and I would feel like I'd been doused in cold water. I wondered how long it would be before that went away.

I looked at Tyler. The funny thing is, he would have been exactly the kind of guy I would have gone for before Nate. I'd always liked the skinny, sensitive, scruffy type. Maybe Tyler was exactly what I needed right now. Maybe if I could just get back to the way I felt before meeting Nate, this horrible weight in my chest would disappear.

"You know what? A date sounds perfect," I told him.

Tyler smiled at me. I tried to ignore how empty it made me feel.

"Great," he said. "I'll meet you in your dressing room."

***

My foray into tabloid land did not end with that one picture. To my horror, I got a call from Jen demanding that I turn on the television that same evening.

"Access Hollywood is talking about you!" she yelled into the phone.

"What?" I asked, dropping the box of macaroni and cheese I had been about to open.

"Turn on the TV, turn on the TV!"

I rushed over to the little television set in my living room and flipped it on. Sure enough, there was a picture of me on the screen. "That's my head shot," I murmured. "Where would they have gotten that?"

"Who cares?" Jen asked impatiently. "They know your name and where you're from. They're saying that the two of you are making a home-town love connection, that he rescued you from obscurity in Detroit!"

"That's ridiculous," I said, shaking my head in bewilderment. "Where the hell are they getting this stuff?"

"Ooh, maybe you have paparazzi outside your apartment *right this minute*," Jen said, sounding entirely too excited about the prospect for my liking.

"Jen," I said. "This is Chicago, not L.A. They don't have paparazzi hanging around on the street corners."

"Oh," she said, sounding disappointed.

I heard the beep indicating call waiting and looked down at the phone. My mom.

"Great," I said to Jen. "My mom is probably watching this too."

"Want to go talk to her?"

"No," I said firmly. "I do not want to get a lecture about how a Hollywood man is not worthy husband material."

"I have to say, you don't sound very excited about this," Jen replied.

"What's there to be excited about?" I asked.

"Being on TV is kind of a big deal," she said. "Especially for someone who wants to be an actress."

"Yeah, but I don't want people thinking I'm in this show because I slept with Jenner."

"Good point. Well, why don't you call him? Maybe his people can do something about it."

I thought about that for a minute. "I don't want to make too big of a deal out of it," I said. "But maybe I'll mention it at the show tomorrow."

"So Ginny tells me everything is going really well," Jen said, and I felt a little pang at the thought of the two of them hanging out without me. Which was totally immature, I know.

"Yeah, we're getting great reviews, tickets are selling well. I might be Broadway bound before you know it."

"That's awesome, hon," she said. There was a pause. "I have to say, you don't sound too excited about that, either."

"No, I am," I said quickly, ignoring the stabbing feeling I got whenever I thought about moving even farther away. "It's a great opportunity."

"You don't have to go," she said quietly. "You know that, right? You can still be an actress without going to New York."

"I know," I said. "But it's a once in a lifetime chance. I'd be stupid to give it up."

"Not if it doesn't make you happy," she pressed.

"Acting makes me happy," I said firmly, determinedly not looking around at the crummy, shabby apartment I was now living in all by myself.

Chapter Twenty-six

"You ready to go?"

I looked up at Tyler, who was standing at the door to the ladies' dressing room.

"Just about," I told him, leaning forward to peer at myself in the mirror. I grabbed a tissue and wiped the last of the red lipstick off my mouth.

"Aw," he said, watching me. "I like you in that shade."

I rolled my eyes as I stood, grabbing my purse. "It's stage make-up. Not exactly subtle."

"Still looks hot on you," he said, winking at me.

There was a time when Tyler's shameless flirting might have made me laugh. Now it just made me feel tired. "So," I said, trying to force myself into the moment as we left the dressing room and headed for the stage door. "Where we headed?"

"I thought we'd go to that pub down the street, get some food. Then we can hit the town. Sound good?"

"Sure," I said, trying to suppress the desire to call the whole thing off and go home. My bed and a pint of ice cream was sounding better and better.

When we reached the pub, I was not at all surprised to find a group of actors and crew members huddled around a table. Though I rarely joined them, I knew this to be a popular post-show hang out.

"Wanna join them?" Tyler asked. "Or—" he leaned closer to me, whispering in my ear—"would you rather have some privacy?"

Though his breath tickled the skin on my neck, I felt nothing from his proximity. No butterflies, no tingles. Just...nothing.

"Let's sit with them," I said, taking a step back.

"Good idea," Tyler said, winking at me. "We can save the privacy for later."

We joined the group at the table, which was overcrowded for my taste. The close quarters seemed to encourage Tyler to sidle up next to me, his hand ever present on my knee.

"So, Annie," a woman named Calllie said, looking me over in an appraising sort of way that immediately made me feel uncomfortable. Callie was new to the show in Chicago, and I hadn't gotten to know her very well. To tell the truth, she kind of seemed like a bitch. "I hear you and Jenner have some hot romance going."

Everyone at the table laughed, and I tried to set my mouth in the general appearance of a smile. "I wouldn't believe everything you read, Callie."

"Well, to be honest, it *was* kind of hard to believe," she said, looking down at my admittedly flat chest. "I mean, you and Jenner."

I was visited with a sudden urge to slap her, but managed to contain myself. Tyler slid his hand a little higher on my leg. "I don't know about that," he said, grinning. "I think Jenner would be lucky to have you."

I laughed along with everyone else, trying to pretend like none of this bothered me.

"Alright," said Bill, the middle-aged man who played my father in the show. "I want to hear who everyone at this table has slept with to get ahead in your career. I'll go first. In 1993 I had a brief but torrid affair with the female producer of a B-list sitcom."

Everyone laughed. "You should be particularly impressed," Bill continued, "seeing as how I'm a raging homo."

"I once slept with a college professor," Tyler said, squeezing my knee under the table. "And she didn't even put me in the show, can you believe it?"

It continued like this for a while, everyone trying to outdo each other with tales of their (hopefully exaggerated) sexual exploits. After a few minutes, I began to lose interest. I was hardly a prude, but even I was feeling uncomfortable with the graphic descriptions flowing freely from these people I hardly knew.

Talk then turned, predictably, to shows people had done and who had worked with whom. I had heard it all before, from these same people, and the bragging was starting to get old. When our food was brought out, I felt immensely relieved that I would have something to distract me with.

"Wow," Callie said, eying my cheeseburger as I raised it to my mouth. "You have quite an appetite, don't you?"

"Mmmhmm," I agreed, taking a huge bite. I'd had about enough of this whole scene.

"You'll want to watch that," she cautioned, adding a miniscule amount of dressing to her salad. "If you want to stay in this business, calories like that definitely aren't your friend."

"Oh well," I said, reaching for my pop. "Guess I better enjoy it while it lasts."

I finished my meal in silence. Tyler tried to draw me into the conversation, but there was no point. A few of these people might have been cool on their own, but put them in a group like this and all anyone cared about with one-upping each other. I thought of Jen and Ginny, wondering what they were up to tonight.

"Wanna get out of here?" Tyler whispered in my ear after our plates had been cleared.

I nodded, eager to be anywhere else.

Tyler threw some bills on the table and we said our goodbyes.

Outside, the cold February air bit against my skin and I huddled down into my coat.

"Let's get a cab," Tyler said, looking over at me.

"Let's just go somewhere close," I said.

"Wouldn't you rather head to a cooler neighborhood? Test out your newfound celebrity and all that?"

I rolled my eyes. "I would rather just be inside."

"There's a bar down here," he said, reaching out and grabbing my hand. "Come on."

We hurried the two blocks to the bar Tyler had in mind. I was hoping for a laid-back place where I could hear myself think, and was somewhat disappointed when we entered a very loud wine bar. There was a live jazz band playing in the back of the room, and a throng of well-dressed professional-looking yuppies standing around talking. I sighed.

"Let's head over here," Tyler said, leading the way to a low couch on the side of the room. There was barely enough room for a single person there, let alone both of us, but he was undeterred, pulling me down next to him so I was practically on his lap.

"There," he said, smiling at me. "That's much better."

I didn't feel much better. In truth, I was feeling pretty damn miserable. I didn't want to go out with Tyler. Why had I thought this would be a good idea?

He gestured to a passing waiter and ordered us both a glass of red. "Unless you'd like a bottle?" he asked me. I shook my head vigorously, already counting down the minutes until I could get out of here without seeming too rude.

"So, you really don't like that crowd, huh?" he asked.

"At the pub?" I asked.

"Yeah. You were so tense in there I could have bounced a quarter off your leg. What was up with that?"

"I just don't like that scene," I told him, shrugging. "I'm not into the bragging and cutting people down."

He shook his head at me. "Sorry to say it, Annie, but you need to toughen up a bit."

I bristled. My nerves, already stretched so tightly, felt ready to snap.

"I just mean," he said, reaching over to rub my shoulder, "that if you want to be in this business, there are certain things you'll have to get used to. How do you think things will be when we get to New York?"

"I don't care where I am," I said flatly. "I can't imagine ever enjoying hanging out with people like that."

"So what will you do, be a hermit forever?"

"I have other friends," I said.

"Yeah, in Detroit. Who do you expect to socialize with in New York?"

"I'll make new friends," I said, my voice skating awfully close to a snarl.

Tyler shook his head. "You have to just embrace this stuff, Annie. If you never hang out with other theater people, how do you expect to get hired? It's all about networking, whether you like it or not. Just like this whole Jenner Collins thing."

"What are you talking about?"

"Well, you're all over the internet today," he pointed out. "Looks like they figured out your name, too."

"Yeah," I told him. "Lucky me."

Tyler smirked. "You are lucky. You might not know it yet, but you are. This will be great for your career. And who knows." He put his arm around my shoulder. "If I stay on your good side, it might be great for my career as well."

I shook his arm off and glared at him. "What are you talking about?"

"Well, it can't hurt to be seen with Jenner Collins' new girlfriend, can it?"

Looking at Tyler's smug, flirty grin, I was suddenly overcome with an emotion very close to revulsion. I didn't think I could sit there with him for another second longer.

"I'm sorry, Tyler," I said, standing. "But this has been a long night. I need to get home."

"What?" he asked, looking up at me incredulously. "You haven't even finished your wine!"

"I'm sorry," I said again, reaching into my purse for a few bills. "I really do have to go."

He looked upset for a minute, then finally rolled his eyes. "Whatever, Annie," he said derisively. "I honestly don't know why I bothered with someone like you anyhow."

For a moment I was temped to ask him what he meant by that, what someone like me was like. I looked down at him and decided it didn't matter. I truly couldn't care less what Tyler, or anyone like him, thought of me.

"Thanks, Tyler," I said softly, before turning to leave.

Chapter Twenty-seven

"So," Jenner said, smiling at me across the table. "How are you handling all of this tabloid nonsense?"

I grinned back. Jenner had asked me to meet him for lunch in his hotel. The restaurant was one of those fancy places that made me feel underdressed no matter what I had on. But at least it was warm in here. I could not say the same for my place.

"It's fine," I told him. "I think I've finally convinced my mom that I'm not moving to L.A. to be your mistress."

He laughed. "I am sorry about all of that. It's one of those things I've grown used to. I almost forget how ridiculous it truly is."

I shrugged. "It's really not a big deal," I assured him. "My best friends from home have taped everything that's been on TV and printed out everything from the internet to put in a scrapbook. So at least it's been fun for someone."

Jenner laughed again, and I smiled. It was funny how comfortable I now felt around him. It had only been a few short months ago when the very sound of his voice on my phone had practically pushed me into a panic attack.

Our waiter appeared with our meals—seared salmon for me, a steak for him—and Jenner thanked him politely. It struck me how nice he always was to the people around him. You would never guess he was a multi-millionaire Hollywood star.

"So, Annie," he said, beginning to cut his steak. "I have a few things I wanted to talk to you about."

I felt my heartbeat quicken. I had assumed that this lunch date was intended only to apologize for the tabloid bullshit, but maybe there was something more. We were only a few weeks away from the scheduled end of our show. We would either move on or shut down. One way or another, this part of my life was almost over.

He pointed at my food with his fork. "Eat!" he urged, smiling.

I grinned and took a bite. The food was delicious but it made me feel a pang for Jen. I hadn't had much besides Raman noodles and mac and cheese since I left our house.

"The show is going to New York," Jenner said casually, before taking another bite of his steak. I stared at him while he chewed. "The producers have asked that we re-cast a few roles, get some bigger names involved."

I wondered briefly if he had brought me here to break the news that I would not be invited to New York. It was the strangest thing—for one moment I felt the strongest rush of relief at the thought.

"They would very much like for you to continue in your role, however," Jenner said.

I stared at him for a moment. "Wow," I whispered. "That's...that's really an honor. Thank you."

He smiled at me. "You've earned it."

I turned back to my food, wondering why I didn't feel more excited. I had not been lying about the opportunity being an honor. To be chosen to originate a role off-Broadway—well, it was a pretty big deal. But I felt no rush of joy, no exhilaration at the thought.

"When will we be going?" I asked.

"That's the other thing I wanted to tell you," Jenner said. "I won't actually be going with you guys."

I looked at him in surprise. "Really? Why not?" I smiled suddenly, remembering our earlier conversation. "Did your agent finally convince you to sign on for another blockbuster?"

He laughed. "Not quite. In fact, my agent is a little upset with me these days." He took another bite of food and I waited again while he chewed. "Do you remember when I told you about my plans for a new company in Detroit?" he finally asked.

I nodded.

"Well, I've just managed to get the last of the funding I need and we've found a space in the city. We've identified a playwright we'd like to work with and we're looking at the summer for our first production. It looks like this is the real deal."

"Holy shit," I whispered, now feeling the excitement that had been missing earlier. A brand new company, right in the city. Knowing Jenner, they'd be finding amazing shows to do. And he had said he wanted to set up an educational component. I could see it all so clearly. "That's going to be amazing, Jenner," I said firmly. "I know it will."

"Thank you," he said. I had the impression he was watching me closely, like he was waiting for something.

"Maybe...maybe when the show is done in New York, I could help out," I said uncertainly, hoping I wasn't overstepping my bounds.

Jenner didn't respond for a moment. I still had the feeling he was waiting for something. "You should definitely call me when you're done. That is, if you don't decide to stay in New York. This show will be pretty big for your resume."

I tried to imagine that. Living in New York and going out on auditions. Another crappy apartment like the one I lived in now. Not knowing anyone except for the same people I'd had dinner with the week before. Going home a few times a year to see the girls. Danny getting big without me.

"I have to say, I'm a little surprised," Jenner said, rousing me from my thoughts.

"About what?"

"I was sure when I told you about the company you'd be begging me to take you back to Detroit," he said, raising his eyebrows at me. "When I told you about it before you seemed so excited. Much more excited then when I told you about New York."

I stared at him. How could he tell?

"Listen, Annie. You're a wonderful actress. I consider you one of the great finds of my career." He met my eyes and I felt a lump form in my throat. It was one of the nicest compliments anyone had ever given me. "You've earned this role and the chance to take it to New York. But I want to make sure you realize something." He held my gaze. "You don't have to leave to be an actress."

I stared down at my plate, unsure of how to respond. It was the same thing I had been telling people my whole life—that I didn't have to leave home to do the thing I loved. But this was New York. This was an opportunity people would kill for...

"I love this play," I told him finally. "It would be make me sick to leave it for someone else to do."

He nodded, and returned to his food.

"Besides," I said, feeling the need to explain myself further. "Besides, how could I ever make people understand? I had a chance to go to New York and I passed it up? No one would ever take me seriously as an actress again."

Jenner was quiet for a moment. "Annie," he finally said, his voice soft. "For a long time I thought that I had to live in L.A. in order to do the work I wanted to do. But I wasn't happy. And honestly..." He paused, and I looked up into his eyes once again. "What the hell is the point of any of this if you aren't happy?"

Chapter Twenty-eight

'There are some women that are afraid to love. Maybe there is some hurt in your past that you've had difficulty getting over. Maybe you're insecure that he will not love you back. In the end, only you can overcome these feelings. Love is the most amazing, precious, reaffirming gift you can receive. Give into it.' —**The Single Girl's Guide to Finding True Love**

After leaving the hotel, I didn't waste any time before calling Ginny. I had my phone to my ear before I'd even gotten into my cab.

"I don't know what to do," I told her as soon as she answered.

"About Nate?" she asked, her voice excited.

"What? No. What are you talking about?" I asked, bewildered.

"Oh...uh, nothing. What were *you* talking about?"

"I don't know if I want to go to New York," I told her. "I mean, that's crazy, right? I have to go. It's New York."

"Did the show get picked up?"

"Yeah. In the spring. I just had lunch with Jenner and he told me I can continue the role if I want to."

"But you don't know if you want to?" she asked.

"No. It would be crazy to say no. I have to go. It's New York."

"Annie," she said. "You don't have to do anything."

"What would you do?" I asked. "If you knew the best place for your career was in New York, what would you do?"

"I'd ask Josh if there was a way we could make it work," she said simply.

"What if he said no? What if the only way you could go is to leave everyone behind?"

"Annie, this is silly," she said. "I can't tell you what to do. Our situations are very different. I can do my job from anywhere. Besides, I'm married. I don't get to make decisions just for me."

"Doesn't that drive you crazy?" I asked, suddenly desperate to understand her thinking. How she could give up so much of herself for her husband? "Taking other people into account? Don't you ever just wish you could do whatever you wanted?"

"No," she said simply. "I really don't. Josh and I have a partnership. I know you think that's cheesy, but it's the best way I can describe it."

I was quiet for a minute. "I think that's the part you never got," she said softly. "That being with someone is not a burden, not when you're right for each other. We don't hold each other back, Ann. We make each other better."

I had no response to that. I wanted to believe her so bad, to believe that it could be that way. Since I was a kid all I had seen of love was how it could hurt you, how it could drain you. How unbalanced it was. In my experience, there was always a winner and a loser.

"It's really not that different from how you and I are, you know?" she continued. "I mean, since Danny came, you and Jen made a ton of decisions that took him into account. Did you resent him for it?"

"He's a baby, Gin," I said. "How could I resent him?"

"No, he's your *family*. And it's no different with me and you. Or me and Josh. Family is worth it."

I took a deep breath, letting her words wash over me. "I should go," I said. "I'm almost home."

"You are?" Her voice sounded funny.

"What?" I asked, immediately suspicious.

"Listen, don't get mad at me," she said in a rush. "I didn't think you would mind, honestly."

"Ginny, what'd you do?"

Before she could respond, the cab was pulling up in front of my apartment. There was a man leaning up against the brick wall of the building, the collar of his wool overcoat pulled high against the cold. It didn't matter that part of his face was covered—I would know him anywhere.

"Ginny, what did you *do*?" I repeated. "Did you give him my address?"

"I'm sorry!" she said. "He called me, I didn't know what else to do. Are you mad? Don't be mad!"

"I have to go," I told her. "The meter's running."

"Call me!" she shouted before I could hang up.

I pulled some bills from my purse and hurriedly paid the cabbie, probably over-tipping in my haste, before climbing out onto the sidewalk, my eyes locked on the man in front of me.

"Hey," Nate said softly.

I felt the strongest urge to burst into tears at the sight of him, but I managed to control myself.

"Hey."

I stared at him for a long moment. He looked so beautiful standing there, outside of my shitty apartment on this shitty street in Chicago.

"Do you...do you wanna come up?" I asked.

"Sure," he said. He hadn't smiled at me, hadn't tried to hug me. Didn't even look at all happy to see me. I had to wonder what he was doing there. Had he come to tell me off? To yell at me about ruining the first chance at happiness I had really had in years?

I opened the front door of my building and led him down the stairs to my apartment. I felt a flash of embarrassment just before I opened the door, but I tamped it down. He had never cared too much about money before. It was silly for me to worry about him judging me now.

"So," I said awkwardly as we stood in the tiny entryway. "Uh, this is my apartment. Why don't you sit down and I'll get us something to drink? I have tea and some really horrible cheap wine."

"I'll take the wine," he said, sitting down on the couch. I winced as he sank low into the broken springs.

I hurried into the kitchen, eager to get a second to clear my head. Seeing him again had shocked me. I felt off-balance and awkward. As I found two plastic glasses and poured out the wine, I realized my hands were shaking.

"Here you go," I told him, rejoining him in the living room and handing him his cup. "Sorry, I don't have many proper dishes. This place is just supposed to be temporary and..." I realized I was rambling and forced myself to knock it off. I contemplated sitting on the couch next to him, but the sagging cushion would only end up making me fall into his lap. I could definitely do without the physical contact at this point.

"So," I said, sitting on the cheap folding chair opposite him. "What brings you out this way?"

"Work stuff," he said. "There's a conference in Chicago this weekend that they sent me to. I figured since I was out here I may as well give you a call."

"I'm glad you did," I said quietly, staring down at my wine.

"Annie," he said. Nothing else. Just my name. He sounded so tired, so weary, like I was exhausting him already. The thought made my heart clench.

"I've missed you," I said, figuring I had nothing to lose. "I've really, really missed you."

"Why?" he asked. "Have you been lonely?" There was an edge to his voice that made me look up. He was staring at me with a hard look on his face. Like he was angry, or impatient.

"No," I said. "I don't miss you because I'm lonely. I miss you because you're you. And it sucks not having you around."

He didn't reply, just looked at me evenly. Like he didn't believe me.

"I missed you too," he said at last. The use of the past tense was not lost on me, and it made my heart drop. That was it then. He was over me.

I gazed at his face, this boy who had been so nice to me, who had seen through all of my pretensions. The first boy who had ever tried to break down my walls, had ever been interested in what was going on inside my heart. This boy that I threw away because I was too scared to accept the fact that he might actually be good to me.

The least I could do is tell him the truth.

"Remember that day in Vegas, when we had first met and we were talking about our families?" I asked quietly.

"Yeah," he said, sounding surprised. "That was our first date. I remember all of it."

I nodded. "You...you told me about your dad and I told you about my parents."

"You were so uncomfortable," he said, shaking his head. "God, I remember looking at you and thinking that it seemed like you thought I was about to arrest you or something. Like you wanted to crawl out of your skin."

I laughed, a short humorless laugh. "Yeah. That's usually how I get when people want to talk about my dad. I try to pretend like it never happened, you know? Because then it can't hurt me."

"You try to pretend like he never left?" he asked, sounding confused.

"No," I said, looking down at my glass again. I didn't want to have to look at his face when I admitted how weak I was. "The leaving was the good part. I try to forget all the stuff that happened *before* he left."

"Like what?" he asked quietly.

"He...he cheated on my mom," I said slowly. "For years. And she knew it. She kept taking him back...or rather, she kept begging him to come back. It was always the same, he would screw around, move in with his girlfriend, and she and I would wait. When she helped me say my prayers at night she would always remind me to ask God to bring my daddy back. I never understand where he was, or why. Not until I got older."

I took a deep breath, determined to keep my voice steady. I never talked about this, not ever. Besides Ginny and Jen, I had never told a soul.

"When I was older, I realized what 'affair' meant. And 'mistress'. I started to get mad at him, so fucking mad. Why the hell was he leaving us that way? Why was he choosing those other women over us? I told my mom I hated him once, and she slapped me. She actually slapped me across the face. It was the only time she had ever hit me. And she did it in defense of the man that was cheating on her."

I shook my head, disgust for her threatening to overwhelm me. "Once she calmed down, she told me that I shouldn't blame him. It was just how men were. That's what she told me. 'All men are like that, Annie.'"

"Ann," he said, his voice tight, but I held up my hand.

"It's not like I believed her," I said quickly. "I know that there are plenty of men who don't cheat. And I didn't expect you to, like, fool around on me or anything like that. I just..."

I paused, at a loss for words. I could feel the tears coming and I was so desperate to hold them off.

"I just didn't want to end up like her," I finally said. "I promised myself that I would never, never end up like her. Wouldn't let my happiness depend on any man, no matter what. She still misses him, can you believe that?" My voice was closing up now, the tears imminent, and I gulped several times. "The last time he left, it was for good. He got remarried, has new kids. And she still wishes, to this day, that he would come back. The day that I...that we...that day in my bedroom I had just gotten off the phone with her. He took her to lunch and she was so excited to tell me about it."

I shook my head as images of my mother's face leapt up in front of my eyes. My poor, stupid mother. Who had loved me and taken wonderful care of me my entire life, even on her own, even under terrible circumstances. She had always wanted only the best for me—and I couldn't even respect her.

"Shit," I whispered, as the tears started to pool. I didn't want him to see me like this, so I stood up quickly.

"I'll be right back," I said, my voice shaking under the strain of my breaking control. "Just need...bathroom—"

Before I could take more than a step, Nate was there, pulling me into his arms. The relief I felt, the happiness at his touch, was so overwhelming I felt my breath catch. But I didn't want him to see me like this. I pulled away.

"Stop," he said, his voice strained. "Annie, please just stop running away from me. Please."

There was so much sadness in his voice. As if my pulling away had literally hurt him.

"Please," he said again, and I finally gave in. I relaxed into his arms, resting my head against his warm chest. And I cried.

I cried for my father, who I had lost so long ago. And I cried for my mom, whose life was so sad. But mostly I cried for me. Because I had let all of these things affect me so much, had let them change me and control me until I could only let my two oldest friends in, no one else.

And I cried because I knew I was in love with this man. And I was scared that he would love me too. Scared of what that would mean and how I would handle it if he did, in fact, love me.

But much more than that, I was scared that he wouldn't.

"I'm sorry," I finally said when my tears had subsided. "I'm sorry I treated you that way."

"It's okay," he said.

"No, Nate, it's not. No one should be treated like that, especially not you. You're too good, way too good to be messed around that way."

"I'm not all that good," he said. "I knew you were hurting but I pushed anyway. I forced you into that decision when I knew you needed more time."

"Please," I said, laughing and pulling away. "Don't try to make me feel better. I'm the bad guy here, okay? Just let me be the bad guy."

"Okay," he said, smiling for the first time since I had laid eyes on him on the street downstairs. The sight of that smile sent my heart lurching somewhere in the vicinity of my ankles. "You're the bad guy."

I laughed—then started crying all over again. "Annie!" he said, looking distraught. "I'm sorry, I was just—"

"Teasing me," I said, smiling through my tears. "I know. I just missed you teasing me, that's all."

"Let me get you a tissue," he said, walking into the bathroom.

I took the opportunity to take deep breaths, trying to calm myself. He returned a moment later and I blew my nose with the proffered tissue.

"Better?" he asked.

"Much." I nodded.

He picked up his wine again and took a drink, taking a glimpse around as he did so.

"Hey," he said, a perplexed expression spreading over his features. "What's with all the boxes?"

"Oh," I said, looking around. I had forgotten about the state of the apartment. "I'm packing. My lease is up in a few weeks."

"Where will you go next?" he asked, looking sad. "Somewhere a little safer, I hope."

I smiled. "Much safer," I said.

"Well, that's good," he said, taking another sip of his wine. "I'm...well, I'm happy to hear it."

We sat in awkward silence for a moment. I had gotten my apology off my chest, and he clearly forgave me, but I had no idea where we stood.

"You know what? This sucks, Annie," he finally said, standing up.

"What?" I asked, surprised at his outburst.

"I came here all prepared to tell you that I was over you. My sisters told me it would be good for me, you know? That I could finally move on if I got some closure. I didn't even need to be at this stupid conference; I volunteered for it because it knew it would get me closer to you." He set his cup down on the coffee table so hard wine splashed out. "And it's been really fucking boring, alright?"

He sounded so annoyed, so frustrated, I almost laughed. I had never seen Nate like this before.

"I'm sorry," I told him, unable to keep the grin off my face. "You could have told me off over the phone, you know, saved yourself the trip."

"Oh, she's so funny," he muttered. "That's Annie, always has a line for everything."

"I'm sorry—"

"No, it's my turn to talk, okay? I let you talk. Now it's my turn."

"Okay," I said, amused. "Go ahead."

"I came here to tell you that I was done, to show you how well I was doing without you. And then I get here and you're standing there outside, looking all pale and freaking beautiful. And then, when I finally get up the courage to say it, you actually open up to me. The thing I've been waiting for since the first day I met you."

I looked up at him in bewilderment, having no idea how to respond to that.

"It's frustrating as hell!" he bellowed.

I had never seen Nate like this before. It was actually really cute, the way his face was getting all red and he kept pushing his blond hair back out of his eyes.

"How in the hell am I supposed to get over you when you keep doing these things to draw me back in, huh?"

I stared at him. Was he actually saying that he still had feelings for me?

"I mean, do you have any idea how much time I've spent waiting for you to call me? To tell me you'd changed your mind and we could give it a go? I would have done that, Annie. Even if you were far away. I think we were worth that. But here you are, all happy in your life in Chicago, apartment-shopping, getting your picture taken all the time with assholes like Jenner Collins. And I'm stuck in fucking Michigan. Where, I might add, we've had about four feet of snow so far this month."

He was really on a roll now, pacing back and forth across my threadbare carpet. I realized that I was grinning broadly, and I tried to cover it, not wanting to piss him off any more. But he was just so adorable like this.

I love him, I thought. *I really, really love him.*

I knew what I wanted to do in an instant, and before I could talk myself out of it, I acted on the impulse. Wanting to stop him before he could get going again, I jumped up from my seat on the folding chair and grabbed his face. He looked at me in surprise for a minute, almost as if he had forgotten I was there.

Without saying a word, I pulled him down to me and kissed him.

I had never really let myself think about what I felt when I kissed him before. I mean, sure, he was an amazing kisser, but I was always trying so hard to ignore the feeling in my chest, like something was expanding, lifting me up out of my shoes. Or the way that my stomach would clench in anticipation when his lips pressed against mine. Or the way it felt like happiness was exploding inside of me when he would sigh against my mouth, when he would cradle my face like it was the most precious thing in the world to him.

I never let myself feel those things before. But I did now. And it was perfect.

"What?" he asked unsteadily, looking down at me. He looked a little dazed, and I had to giggle. "What was that?"

"I'm in love with you," I told him. "I am. And even though that scares the hell out of me, I wanted you to know it."

"You're in love with me?" he asked.

"Of course I am," I said, kissing the corner of his mouth. "You knew that. You knew it before I did."

He looked at me in that dazed way for another minute, before he started laughing. "Are you serious?"

Then he was kissing me again, and spinning me around, and it was all very cheesy and romantic. The kind of thing I normally would have rolled my eyes at.

But I wasn't rolling my eyes now.

"Put me down," I finally said, hitting him. "Get a hold of yourself, man. This is no way for a tough guy to act. What are you, a woman?"

"Shut up," he growled, pulling me close. "You love me. So any insults you want to hurl, just remember: you're the fool that loves me."

"Hmm, you have a good point," I said. "Maybe I'll have to stop teasing you altogether."

"Oh no, Annie," he said seriously. "Please don't ever do that."

He pulled me down onto the couch with him, situating me in his lap as the cushions sagged under me.

"Ooof, I certainly hope your new place has better furniture then this. I mean, I can hardly be expected to jet my ass all the way over here every weekend and sit in this pile of springs."

I snuggled up into his chest. "What do you mean jet your way over here?" I asked.

"To Chicago," he said. "To see you."

"Oh, I won't be in Chicago," I said. "Didn't I explain that?"

"No," he said, looking down at me. "Are you...are you guys going to New York?"

"The show is," I said. "But I'm not."

Nate just stared at me in disbelief. "But...but, why? Annie, this is your dream—"

"No, it's not," I said firmly. "My dream is to make a living as an actress. New York was never my dream; I just went along with it because it seemed to be what everyone expected."

"But—"

"I'm unhappy here, Nate," I said. "I have been the entire time. Not just because I missed you. I'm unhappy because I don't like the people that I work with. I'm unhappy because I can only afford this little shithole. I'm unhappy because I'm not with my friends. I miss my home."

"But what will you do?" he asked. "Go back to working in an office at Springwells? You were so unhappy there."

"No," I said firmly. "I'll keep auditioning. In fact, Jenner is starting a regular company up in the city. It's small, but he's really committed to it. And there's no guarantee I'll get a place with them, but I'll try. I mean, at least I have more experience now, you know, for my resume. It's worth a shot."

Nate didn't say anything, and I felt my heart sink a little. "What?" I asked. "Are you not happy that I'm coming home?"

"No," he said, pulling me close. "The thought of you so close to me is... well, let's just say that would make me really freaking happy. But I don't want you to do something that you'll end up regretting. Especially not for me."

I laughed. "Sorry, babe," I told him. "But there's no way in hell I'm doing this for you, or for anyone else. Do you know who you're talking to here?"

He rolled his eyes and rested his forehead against mine. "I must have forgotten. This is Annie-I-make-my-own-decisions-all-the-time."

"You just said you didn't want me making this choice over you!" I cried, slapping his shoulder.

"Well, not entirely. But you could factor me in a little, you know. Just some of the time."

I thought about what Ginny had told me, about how a good relationship should be a partnership. How you should take the other person into account, but only if they did the same with you. A balance.

"Maybe I could do that," I said, leaning forward to kiss him again. "Just some of the time."

Chapter Twenty-nine

*'There's one important thing about true love that you should always keep in mind: when it's right, it's right. You can memorize all the dating tips and rules in the world, but when it's true love, everything will eventually come easily. Never forget the relationships that got you where you are, and made you who you are. Even the ones that seemed tragic at the time helped make you who are you are now, the woman your true love can't live without.'—**The Single Girl's Guide to Finding True Love.***

"Hey," I said, peeking around the door into Jenner's office. "I'm gonna take off, okay?"

"Go, go," he said, making a shooing motion with his hands. "You should have left an hour ago. Your man will be pissed."

I rolled my eyes. "He can deal with it. Do you have directions?"

He patted his pocket. "Right here in my phone," he said. "See you in a few hours."

I waved and headed back down the hallway, stopping in my office to grab my bag and turn off the light. There was a stack of papers on my desk for the new playwriting classes, but it could wait until Monday. Nothing I couldn't handle.

Outside, I unlocked my bike from the streetlight pole where I had secured it that morning. Being close enough to ride to work was definitely one of the major perks of my new situation.

Before I could jump on the seat, my phone rang. I looked down at the screen and smiled. Jen. I had been expecting this call—was, in fact, amazed she'd managed to contain herself for so long.

"What is it now?" I asked.

"You're late!" she said in her stressed-out voice. "I have a million things for you to do!"

"Keep your shirt on," I told her. "I'm on my way, okay?"

"Fine," she said, sighing. "But you better hurry. It's your party, you know?"

"I know, and I appreciate all of your work," I told her with a grin, feeling a rush of fondness for my type-A best friend.

I pressed the end button and climbed onto my bike. It was a warm day, perfect May weather, and I enjoyed the sensation of the breeze on my skin as I peddled the short distance home.

"Hey," Nate called from the porch as I approached. He was balancing a white box in his arms, but he waited for me to pull my bike up the steps so he could kiss me hello. "You're late."

"So I keep hearing," I said, giving him a second kiss for good measure. "What's in the box?"

"Cupcakes," he said.

"She's sending you out for cupcakes now?" I asked.

"She would have sent you, had you been here."

I grinned. "Oops. I hope you don't have any false ideas that I might have planned this to avoid doing Jen's errands."

Nate rolled his eyes. "Sure you didn't. How about you open the door? This is a little heavy, you know."

I opened the door to our house and let him walk in ahead of me. "Hello!" I called out. "I'm home!"

"It's about time," Jen said, appearing in the doorway to the kitchen. "Nate, take those into the dining room, there's a dessert table by the window."

I rolled my eyes at him as he passed and he sighed dramatically.

"Don't be so bossy," I told Jen. "You're the one who wanted to do all this. We would have been happy with pizza and beer."

"You need a proper house-warming party," she said. "This is a huge deal, Annie!"

"I know," I told her, walking past her into the kitchen to grab a water. "Whoever would have thought that I'd be living with a boy?"

"Not me," she muttered.

"Be nice!" I told her. "I could still change my mind and move back to Ferndale with you and Matt."

"Not a chance," Nate said, coming up behind me and wrapping his arms around my waist. "You signed a mortgage, baby. You're stuck with me."

"I guess I am," I said, smiling. "Poor me."

***

Three hours later, the party was in full swing and our house was full.

"I love this place," Matt was saying to Josh as the two of them examined the oak banister. "The architecture is so cool. All this woodwork? I bet it's original to the house." As I passed them, I caught a glimpse of Jen rolling her eyes behind his back. I smiled at her, but to be honest, I was on Matt's side on this one.

I had never thought I'd care too much about the kind of house I lived in, but once Nate and I started looking, I found that there was an undiscovered real estate fanatic buried deep inside. I was particularly fascinated with the old Victorians that dotted this area of Detroit and it was no surprise that we ended up in one. Nate and I had looked for ages before settling on this house. It was much too big for just the two of us, but I loved it anyhow. From the woodwork, to the original claw foot tub, to the turret attic room, it was the most perfect house I could imagine.

"Hey, Annie," a voice hissed in my ear.

I turned and saw Emily, Nate's sister, hovering at my elbow. She had come in for the week to check out our new place and spend some time with her big brother. I had been relieved to find that she and I got along really well. I knew that it made Nate happy.

"Is that Jenner Collins over there?" she whispered, pointing into the dining room.

I squinted in that direction and saw Jenner with a stunningly pretty blond woman at his side.

"Yup," I said. "And that girl with him is Melinda Berry. You know, from that sitcom, *Sisters*?"

Emily gasped. "Wow! Oh my God. I can't believe I'm in the same room as Melinda Berry. And Jenner Collins! This is so cool!"

I grinned at her. "Go find your brother," I told her. "He'll introduce you."

"Look at you," Ginny said, coming up next to me as Emily scurried off. "Making nice with the in-laws."

I rolled my eyes. "You have to be married to have in-laws," I pointed out.

"Still," she said, putting her arm around me. "I'm proud of you."

"Why are you proud of *her*? I'm the one who planned this whole thing," Jen said, joining us.

"I wasn't talking about the party," Ginny said. "I was talking about Annie's emotional growth."

"Oh, that. Yeah, I'm proud of that too."

"Oh, shut up," I told them. "You make it sound like I was a basket case or something."

"We're just happy that you're happy," Jen said, putting her arm around me as well. "You are happy, aren't you?"

I thought about that. At that precise moment, tired was probably the best word for how I was feeling. I had been working long hours at The Brush Theater, Jenner's new company. I had a supporting role in the first production, set to open in July. Beyond that, I was working my ass off to get the education department set up, as well as helping out to get the artist-in-residence program off the ground. It was exhausting work, but I wouldn't change it for anything.

Most of my spare time had been going into this house. Like many of the places on the street, this one had been a real dump when we first found it. But a lot of renovation was happening on this block. Like many of our neighbors, we were determined to bring our home back to its former glory. It was a work in progress, but I was very happy with all we had done so far. And who would have guessed that I would actually enjoy things like stripping hard wood floors, or re-tiling kitchens?

I caught sight of Nate across the room, leaving his gushing sister with an amused-looking Jenner, and I smiled. To tell the truth, I would probably enjoy just about any chore so long as I got to do it with Nate.

"Oh my God," Ginny said, laughing. "If you could see the look on your face right now!"

"What?" I said.

"You're smiling like a lovesick teenager."

"Oh, I am not," I said, feeling embarrassed.

"You are," Jen agreed. "Don't worry, it's cute. And we won't tell anyone."

"So I guess that answers Jen's question," Ginny said. "You are happy, aren't you?"

"I am," I said.

Across the room, I saw my mom chatting with Mrs. Campbell. My dad had hung around for a few months, taking her out every once in a while and hinting that he might like a reunion. I hadn't heard about him in a few weeks now, and I wondered if he had disappeared again. Or maybe she'd actually done the unthinkable and told him to get lost. I could hope.

"What if it doesn't last?" I whispered. It was my biggest fear, one I didn't even like to talk to Nate about, but I could ask the girls. They would understand. "What if something goes wrong?"

"Then we'll help you fix it," Ginny said, releasing my shoulder and reaching over to grab my hand. "No matter what happens with Nate, we'll be here, Annie. The same way we always have been."

I squeezed her hand back, believing her. It was the one thing in my life I had never doubted.

The three of us stood like that for a long moment, watching the friends and family who had gathered to help celebrate my new home. Out of the corner of my eye, I saw Nate now approaching Josh and Danny. He reached out and patted Danny's head, saying something to him that made the baby laugh. Ginny squeezed my hand again.

Watching Nate, I felt warmth spread throughout my chest, bringing certainty with it. I had a feeling I had finally found something else that I didn't have to doubt.

ABOUT THE AUTHOR

Rachel Schurig lives in the metro Detroit area with her dog, Lucy. She loves to watch reality TV, and she reads as many books as she can get her hands on. In her spare time, Rachel decorates cakes.

To find out more about the books in this series, visit Rachel at http://rachelschurig.com

CPSIA information can be obtained at www.ICGtesting.com
Printed in the USA
LVOW12s2336230114

370707LV00006B/583/P